What You
ee Is What
You Get

What You See Is What You Get

ROSEMARY FURBER

WOLFHOUND PRESS

First published in 2004 by
Wolfhound Press
An Imprint of Merlin Publishing
16 Upper Pembroke Street
Dublin 2, Ireland
Tel: + 353 1 6764373
Fax: + 353 1 6764368
publishing@merlin.ie

Text © 2004 Rosemary Furber
Design and Layout © 2004 Merlin Publishing

ISBN 0–86327–924–4

A CIP catalogue record for this book is available from the British Library.

5 4 3 2 1

Typeset by Carrigboy Typesetting Services
Cover design by Faye Keegan Design
Printed and bound in Denmark, by Nørhaven Paperback A/S

Acknowledgements

With thanks to
my editor Aoife Barrett,
my sons Robert and Charlie,
my husband James who kept the spirits flowing
and above all
my daughter Biz who kept my spirits up.

Chapter One

Tim locked the toilet door and laid his camera, note-book and pencil on the window ledge. The frosted window was crusted stiff, so he wrapped his sweat-shirt sleeve round his fist, gave it a nudge and leant outside. It was still cloudy out there, very cloudy. The removal van was taking up most of the path below. It would have been a path with great skateboarding potential if some idiot hadn't covered it with gravel. Tim could hear shouting – Mum and Dad giving each other orders and ignoring them. No sign of Rox or Georgie, probably both hiding in case they were asked to help.

The removal men were leaning on boxes all over the grass, drinking coffee and staring at the sky. At least they had some sense. That was what everybody should be doing, today of all days. Who would want to move into a new place on the day of the total eclipse of the sun? Tim was not going to miss watching it.

He had a plan. He was going to write down every-thing he saw and take one photograph every fifteen minutes to record the change of light. No chance of the sun disappearing completely in Greenwich. Between two and five solar eclipses a year, it said in his book, but not where he lived and the next one wouldn't be until 2090.

10.03 and 30 seconds, he wrote. *First Contact. Cloudy.*
Somebody tried the door handle.

"Mum wants you!"

Rox. By 2090 she would, with any luck, be very far away from Tim. Or dead.

"We know you're in there!" she yelled.

Tim flushed the loo and sat on the lid. They could manage without him.

"It's no use pretending," Rox bellowed.

Tim faked a straining noise.

"If you don't come and help," she said, "I'll get the best bedroom."

She would anyway. There was no standing between Rox and the best of everything. She gave the door a shove and it fell open.

"Leave me alone," Tim said, and tried to flush the loo again. The handle flapped in his hands.

Rox came straight in and looked out the window. "You can't see from here anyway. What've you got there?" she asked, snatching Tim's notebook. "First Contact," she read, "what's that?" As if she didn't know.

"When the orbit of the moon puts it in conjunction with the sun . . ."

"Oooh," she cut in, "blind me with science."

"It's the moment they begin to overlap."

"Where?" she asked.

"Behind that cloud. The big one, there."

"So that's where the feminine moon is caressing the masculine sun . . . "

Tim was tempted to stuff a loo roll down her stupid throat. They're nearly 150 million kilometres apart,

2

he wanted to shout. It only looks as if they're touching. But she was droning on

". . . if negative forces weren't clouding it up?"

"It's August, clouds are normal," Tim said but Rox had fallen to her knees, clasping his notebook to her chest: "Oh Universe! Help the good in heart to combine in a plea for a sign," she chanted.

She really had been reading some very peculiar stuff recently.

"Look!" she yelled, as a drop of rain fell on the window pane. "It's working!"

"It's only rain," Tim said.

"Don't be so negative," Rox pouted and suddenly jumped on him. Tim clung to the door, as she tried to tug him out onto the landing, shouting, "I've found him!" Her yell echoed down the circular stone staircase.

She let go and started to dangle his notebook over the banister. He hated it when she made him feel like this – as if he could kill her. He was about to put her in a headlock when she went rigid.

"What's that noise?" she whispered.

"One of the men."

"They're all downstairs."

"Give me my notebook."

Rox laughed and went "Got you!" and dangled the notebook over the banister again.

"GIVE IT!" Tim roared. He rushed at her again and felt her arms closing horribly tight around him. *New place*, he thought, *same old problem*. Rox had only one defect – she was insufferable. Before he had time

3

to work out a strategy she had bent him backwards over the banister. She was at least a stone heavier than he was and his head was pulsing with blood and panic. If she pushed him right over he could die. Then he heard the notebook clatter onto the stone slabs in the hall below.

Suddenly she flopped away from him.

"You heard it this time," she shouted, "you did!"

"Heard what?"

She was staring down at the notebook splayed on the hall floor.

"A voice, a man yelling *ADMIT IT*' and then something fell."

"My notebook."

"No, it was heavy. Something heavy fell, hitting the floor. Down there."

As she turned to Tim and swallowed, her lips were very pale. Her whole face was chalk white.

Tim pulled his clothes straight and gave her his head-on-a-spike face. He knew her tricks and wasn't fooled. He knew he had heard nothing.

Chapter Two

"Well, I thought the best thing about the eclipse," Mum boomed, "was the silence. Even the birds shut up and I'd like some silence now!"

It had started simply enough. Rox had been doodling a dragon on her pizza box and holding forth about how people used to believe that the sun was being eaten up.

"The Vietnamese thought the sun was this huge frog and the Chinese saw a dragon, that they thought they had to scare away with drums and rockets and stuff. Isn't that just brilliant?"

Tim explained how ridiculous that was as the sun always came back anyway.

"Well, during an eclipse in the twenty-second century BC," Rox shouted over him, "the Chinese emperor had two astronomers beheaded for being drunk on duty."

That was when the row had started. Rox amazed Tim sometimes. First the feminine moon. Now dragons. If scientists were trying to design the ultimate idiot, they could use her as the blueprint.

"What we have here is a personality clash," Rox muttered.

"Yeah," Tim said. "I've got one and you haven't."

"Quiet!" Dad yelled. "Your mother and I want to eat in peace." He raised his glass to Mum and she raised hers back. "To our new home, darling. May we have the strength . . ."

"And the money," Mum chipped in.

". . . to make it the home of our dreams."

They smiled.

"For the first time in our lives we've got a place we can do up exactly as we like," Mum said, "and it's going to be gorgeous. Come on, glasses everybody. Hang on, where's Georgie? Georgie!"

Georgie crawled out from under the table. His arm was round a scruffy, four-legged toy with no nose. Mum stroked one of its floppy ears.

"Well hello there, Lamby," she said, "I thought Georgie had grown out of you years ago."

Georgie gripped Lamby tighter and disappeared back under the table.

Mum looked worried but let him go.

"So much for the toast," Tim muttered as Mum took Rox's hand on her right. She told Tim and Dad to stop grinning and to join hands around the table. Tim was wondering what was going on when he realised that Rox must have told her about the weird voices. Mum closed her eyes, looking mysterious.

"Let the séance begin," Tim whispered.

"Is there anybody there?" Mum sang in a spooky voice. "Knock once for yes . . . and twice for no."

Georgie knocked the underside of the table – twice.

Tim couldn't say why but, even though he was laughing, this made his stomach jump a bit. Ever since their first visit to the abbey he'd been unsure about the place. Mum kept saying weren't the vibes just

6

perfect and the estate agent had droned on about anterooms and architraves until Dad asked him exactly what an architrave was and he shut up. But Mum knew. She'd told them all later that architrave was just a fancy word for a door frame. She knew because she'd always wanted to live somewhere glamorous enough for a brilliant, if so far under-valued, actress like herself. Castles were all impossibly expensive but an abbey would do. Especially if the abbey was a cheap one burnt down and rebuilt like this one, with precious little in it that the original monks would have recognised. So when Grandpa's cancer finally squeezed the last breath out of him and Gran wasn't doing at all well on her own, the decision was made. The flat in Greenwich Abbey was cheap because so much had to be done to it, Gran would have her own little flat downstairs and the rest of them would have more room than ever before upstairs. So that was that.

Now that they had arrived though, Tim was not the only one who was unsure. Mum was complaining that the kitchen was so small that she could only boil one egg at a time and Georgie was laboriously wiping his feet *before* he went out.

But that was not what was on Rox's tiny mind as the séance broke up.

"Mum," she said, "Tim took forty pictures today and not one of them was of me. Not one!" Whatever he did, she tried to hijack it.

"It's a scientific record," Tim muttered, "not a clothes show."

"Show me," Mum said. She leaned over and planted a pizza thumbprint in the middle of the first of his precious Polaroid photographs.

"These are lovely, darling," she said, "all the umbrellas in the park. Look at those removal men not doing a stroke of work. And who's that?" She passed the photo to Dad.

"More to the point what's she wearing?" Dad coughed to cover a laugh. "Whatever it is, it needs ironing."

"Tony," Mum nudged Dad's arm, "she's ... "

"What? What?" Rox leaned over Georgie who'd come out to have a look.

He glared at her. "It's not Gran, is it?" he asked.

"No," Mum said, "she stayed in all day. Said she wasn't bothered with eclipses without Grandpa. I caught her putting his shirts in a drawer. She told me last week she'd given them away." Mum was looking even more worried.

"I'll go and find Gran," Georgie offered.

"No you sit down and eat. Rox can go," Mum said.

But Rox had spread the photographs around her plate and was leaning back laughing. "That woman hasn't got a stitch on!" she giggled.

"Give them here," Mum growled. But Tim got there first. The photos were his after all. He had a good look. There was the removal van in the gloom of the eclipse with orange street lights in the background. In the lower left corner there was a grainy back view of, yes it really seemed to be, an old woman stark naked, kneeling down on the path.

8

Tim clenched his teeth so he wouldn't laugh too. "What's she doing?"

"Obvious," Rox giggled, "she's praying for the sun to come back."

Mum was just getting up to go and get Gran herself when there was a tap on the back door and Gran came in, looking flustered.

"Hey, Gran," Rox called. "Look at this, don't you think she's praying? To the sun."

Gran looked briefly and said, "Very nice, dear. We've got a visitor."

A small chubby man in a green blazer picked his way through the boxes before offering to shake Mum's hand.

"MacFadyen. Magnificent windows."

"No double-glazing, thanks," Mum replied, folding her arms.

The man shoved his half-moon spectacles up his nose. "Absolutely not. These windows are architectural jewels. You're much more fortunate than your neighbours." He pointed in the direction of the only other inhabited flat. "Their windows are modern rubbish if you ask me."

"And why are next door's windows any of your business?" Gran asked.

Rox butted in, "That's Mrs Baldock's. We haven't met her yet." Rox was still giggling at the photographs, "Oh my God, do you think it's her?"

Mr MacFadyen slid a page from his clipboard and handed it to Gran.

"I dare say next door's is a sight neater than in here though, mm?" he said.

"You dare say?" Gran muttered and passed his page to Mum without reading it.

"Neater?" Mum was fuming, "We've just moved in, how could we be neat? I'll show you neat!"

Mum folded Mr MacFadyen's page and tucked it into his blazer pocket.

Dad looked up.

"And who might you be anyway?" he asked.

Mr MacFadyen looked outraged.

"My job, Madam, Sir, is to check that people doing up old buildings don't throw away all the beautiful old things that should be kept and treasured. *I am not used to being treated in this manner,*" he said. Then he walked very slowly to the front door and slammed it behind him.

"Show's over," Mum said and set about ushering the children up to bed. Tim had a feeling that wouldn't be the last they'd see of the funny, little man and his clipboard.

Chapter Three

Tim was heading his football into the air for the fourteenth time in a row and hoping Mrs Cox would notice. It was odd to be back in the school playground in the holidays, especially on a Saturday, but the football warm-up was the best reason he could think of. After all the hassle of the move it was good to know that some things stayed the same.

Suddenly, without any warning, an arm swung round his neck from behind and pressed so hard into his throat, it was about to crack. He could hardly breathe.

Same school with the same old problems. Everyday last term Big Danny's lot had got him. Tim never knew when it was coming but it always came, and every time it happened Tim had felt stupid as well as deeply frightened. The arm yanked tighter. It had the distinctive feel of Pitbull Pete, who liked wrestling that way with his ugly dog.

Mrs Cox seemed to have disappeared. Nobody else said anything. They kept their heads down and started moving away. Big Danny rolled in front of Tim, stopped and flicked his skateboard up into his hand.

"What'd I see you doing yesterday?"

"When? Where?" Tim croaked.

"In the park. With wheels on."

"You mean my skateboard?" he gasped. Tim's skateboard had only turned up the day before, among the saucepans. Tim couldn't help it. He looked over at his board waiting against the wall to take him home. They wouldn't steal it, would they?

Danny strolled over and with a swerve of his toecap brought Tim's board crashing to the ground.

"Call that a skateboard?"

Danny's loud laughter ricocheted off the wall.

"I've seen girls on better skateboards than that. You get it down the dump?" Big Danny sneered.

"Iitt'ss . . ." Pete's stranglehold was making Tim croak, "I bought it. Off the internet."

Danny stamped in a puddle wetting Tim's trousers and feet.

"Wanna see a real skateboard, Timmy? Eh?"

A woman's laugh floated across the playground. It was Mrs Cox over by the school gate trying to impress somebody's Dad. Danny looked over at her too, then pulled Tim's glasses off and waved them above his shaven head. Big Danny's breath smelled of smoke. His teeth shone yellow like a rat's, as he grinned and shoved his skateboard in Tim's face. It was black and covered in skulls, with glinting metal around the edges, as though blades were concealed inside.

"See that, Timmy? Quality."

Tim felt himself being lifted off the ground by the neck. His face swelled up, all hot.

"I said did ya see it, Timmy?"

Tim tried to shout but Big Danny's boot swung his feet aside and all Tim could do was land hard on his side and elbow. Everything was wet and cold and very dark. Big Danny burst out laughing as he carefully placed Tim's glasses back on his face and skimmed away down the playground.

Tim was still on the ground when he heard Mrs Cox clapping as she came back. "Come on, you lot," she shouted. "I leave you for one minute and everybody stops dead. Tim Exworth get up. This is no time for having a rest."

*   *   *

Tim lay on his bed. He was thinking about Big Danny. He didn't want to think about him but every time his mind had nothing much to do, like now in the half-hour before dinner, worries about Big Danny overwhelmed him. If only, some day, somehow, Big Danny would drop dead. Tim watched his left fist punch a graceful arc into the safety of his right palm. *He* would never have the nerve to *hit* Big Danny of course. He'd never have the nerve to hit anybody. Except maybe Rox.

"WOOOoooohhhhh."

He turned to the doorway and saw two blue caterpillars standing there, one tall and one short, giggling.

"What do you two want?"

"We're ghosts. WOOOoooohhhhh. Aren't we frightening?"

"Ghosts don't wear sleeping bags over their heads. It's a well-known fact," Tim growled.

Roxanne poked her head out of her sleeping bag and waddled into Tim's room.

"This place is haunted, you know," she said. "Bound to be. We've come to get you used to the idea just in case a ghost comes after you in the night."

13

"It won't."

"How do you know? Think of all those monks who've lived here over the centuries. All those souls who've died here – maybe in this very room . . ."

Georgie's head poked out of his sleeping bag with huge eyes.

"Stop it you're scaring Georgie. There's no such thing as ghosts. Everything has a scientific explanation," Tim said and found his *Everything Explained* book. It explained everything except why he, Tim, was born with such an annoying, pig-faced sister.

"Wouldn't that be nice?" she smirked. "But I don't believe it. Even you don't believe it. Because it's not true. What does your precious book say? Give it here. What does it say about . . . ghosts? Let's see. Typical! They're not even in the index. Spectres? Supernatural? Witches? Walking through walls? Not a thing."

"They'll be under D for daft."

Georgie laughed and rolled his eyes.

"Explain this then. My friend Alice saw a figure cross her room one night and her Mum swears she's smelt a strange smell in their house."

"All in the mind. Especially in the stupid girly mind, if I may say so. As far as we scientists . . ."

"Ooooh!" Rox sang.

". . . as far as we scientists are concerned," Tim went on, "one rule applies and one rule only – WYSIWYG."

"Wizziwig?" Georgie giggled.

"Yep. WYSIWYG. Stands for What You See Is What You Get. It's in computers: what you see on the screen is what you get on the page. Same with ghosts. What you see in the daylight when you're wide awake with your eyes open is all there is. Do you see anything peculiar in this room, apart from you two? No. You've both got perfectly good rooms of your own that probably have better ghosts in them too. So get *out* of my room. Now."

Rox was looking insufferably smug as her room was much bigger than Tim's, with a balcony and a view of Greenwich Park.

"We can't. We're here on a mission," she smirked. "We bring you a message from the other side."

"The other side of the flat? The only good thing about *this* room is that *yours* is so far away!"

Rox was undaunted.

"Woooooooohhh – woooooooohhh!" She was waving her arms and making Georgie sing along. "Woohoo!" Had they no idea how stupid they looked?

Mum was thumping up the stairs. Rox and Georgie panicked and fell down in a pile and then wriggled away to their rooms. Tim rolled off and hid under his bed. He knew what was coming next.

"If I have to mention tidying again," Mum yelled, "there'll be big trouble. Rox? Georgie? I know you're up here!"

Tim's door was flung open.

"And the same goes for you too, young man," Mum said. We've been here less than a week and already this room is *disgusting*. No tea unless you make a start. And I know you can hear me under there. I can hear your tummy rumbling." She slammed out of the room again.

Tim stood up. His room looked fine to him. In fact it felt very good to have a room of his own at last. Even if it only had one little window facing north and looked out at nothing but big, dark trees. It had all Tim wanted — a door he could shut and be peacefully by himself.

He knew where things were too, except for the stuff that still hadn't turned up since the move. No sign of his spare specs for one thing, but his comics were safely under the bed, with the socks he'd worn but didn't want washed yet and his dinosaur bones.

Roxanne said his dinosaur bones were old chicken bones mixed up in the garden compost by mistake but Tim knew better. He'd written to the Natural History Museum seventeen days ago with samples, measurements and some of his drawings. No reply yet but the dinosaur expert had probably replied to their old address. He could smell the dinosaur bones, just thinking about them.

Tim picked up a sweet paper, put it in his pocket to look willing and scratched his nose. The bone smell was getting worse. Maybe if he wrapped them in the socks, they'd smell better. He stretched his hand under the bed and felt through the fluff. He came across the occasional rolled sock but there was no sign of the bones. Where could they be? Had Rox stolen them? The best thing to do, the only thing really, was to lie down on his bed again and have a think. He left the door open in case Mum came back.

As Tim lay back into his pillow and closed his eyes, the bed tilted as if somebody was sitting there beside him. Somebody quite fat who was a bit smelly Somebody who hadn't had a bath in a while . . .

He sat up and opened his eyes. The bed levelled out again but quick as he was, Tim couldn't see anybody. He was completely alone.

Chapter Four

The front door banged shut downstairs and Tim's room juddered.

Whoever had sat on his bed was not getting away, Tim thought. He sprinted down the old stone staircase imagining he was on his skateboard executing a perfect frontside nosegrind. He skidded to a halt against his dad who'd just come in. He was putting his change in three neat piles, the way he always did, and laying his train season ticket at right angles between them.

"Hello, old man," he said.

Tim swerved past him and shot out the door.

"Come back here!" Dad shouted. "I want a proper welcome. I want happy shouts of Dad's Home! Where're Rox and Georgie?"

Tim searched the garden for his bedroom visitor but nobody was there. Georgie was worming down the stairs and Rox was gliding down, trying to look poised and superior, as he went back inside.

"Dad," Tim said, "did you see anybody as you came in?"

"Nope. Where's your mother?"

Mum came out from the kitchen complaining that the kitchen cupboards had been torn out that day and nothing put back yet and she'd spent the whole day nearly in tears. Dad said he knew the feeling, he would tell her later.

"Right dinner everyone," Mum shouted, looking even more stressed out.

Mum was busy sharing out the Chinese takeaway when Dad poured himself a glass of wine and cleared his throat.

"Once upon a time there were three little piggies who all worked together in a stinky little office," he said. "One day they all had a special meeting. They decided their little piggy office wasn't doing very well and one of them would have to leave."

Rox sat up, suddenly interested. "Was this special meeting on a Saturday? Like today?" she asked.

Dad ignored her.

'"We needn't decide today,' said the oldest little piggy, 'but in three months, we'll all meet again and by then we'll know which one of us will have to leave and go alone out into the big wide world.' Then they all had piggy coffee and piggy biscuits . . . "

"Chocolate biscuits?" Georgie asked.

"The piggies like chocolate ones but they can't afford them. It's a sad story but I hope it'll have a happy ending. And in three months' time I'll tell you the rest."

"It's about you, isn't it, Dad?" asked Rox.

Dad laid a finger secretively on the side of his nose. Tim caught his eye but Dad looked away first. Something was seriously wrong.

*   *   *

After dinner Tim ran upstairs two at a time as usual. He was rehearsing his booster talk for the school's

First Team. Not that he was captain yet. He was waiting to hear if he was even going to be in the team, but some day . . .

He started shouting, "It's all about morale! You can't see it or touch it or weigh it but when it comes to football it's the most valuable stuff in the world . . ."

He pushed open his bedroom door and there was Rox, in the act of stealing his rubber. Tim's response was so loud it surprised them both, "OUT OF MY ROOM!"

Rox rested her fists on her hips and opened her mouth to speak.

Tim decided to appeal for once to her powers of reason. "Listen carefully, Rox. Put the rubber down and get out. If you don't, I'll kill you."

Mum clattered upstairs. She was always doing that at the first sound of anybody defending themselves.

"Roxanne! Own room, now!"

"I can't stand the stink in here anyway," Rox said and flounced away.

"Tim!" Mum shouted. Was he about to get the full half-hour lecture? "This room is the worst!"

What? Had she seen Rox's room lately? Like a skip outside a junk shop.

"Pick up those socks," Mum said. She rubbed her forehead so that the worry lines went up and down. "And try and do something about that awful smell."

She did have a point about the smell.

*   *   *

Tim was dreaming . . . *he had just scored a clincher for Manchester United and was grinding along the top of the goal mouth on his skateboard with the roar of applause in his ears. He could feel the heat of the spotlights full on his face. One spotlight. Very close to his face. Wavering. Like a candle . . .*

He opened his eyes to total darkness and switched on the light in his watch. 1.03 a.m. A gale was blowing the branches almost flat outside his window. Gusts blew down his chimney and battered against the sheet of hardboard covering the fireplace. An eerie half-light began to outline Tim's piles of this and that, as his eyes grew used to the gloom. As clearly as he saw the wall itself, he saw a lumpy bundle of clothing lying on the end of his bed. He sat up.

Very slowly, as if in pain, the bundle expanded and rose to the height of a man.

"Who are you?" Tim whispered.

The moment Tim spoke the figure began to disappear. It started from the outside into the middle, until for the last second, nothing was left but hands with long, sturdy fingers wriggling over and around each other like slimy worms.

Tim knocked himself twice on the head with his knuckles. *Funny sort of dream*, he thought.

* * *

Next morning he actually called Rox into his room. She listened with more seriousness on her face than Tim had ever seen there before.

21

"I knew it," she said.

"Don't talk rubbish."

"You don't ever think that you, the almighty scientist, might sometimes be wrong?"

"And you're never wrong, I suppose," Tim muttered. "WYSIWYG, remember? What you see is what you get. It was a dream."

He wished he'd never brought it up.

Rox ran a finger along his bedside table.

"Maybe the ghost came to clean up. Did it make your mirror any shinier?"

Tim went over to look at his reflection. He looked the same as he always did in the morning. His hair up on end like a dog's ears and that gap at the side there where his new tooth was taking ages to grow. He couldn't remember what the mirror had looked like before.

"Don't think so," he said.

"Forget it then. It was just a dream," Rox agreed. She was still trying to forget the scary 'Admit It!' voice. She was starting to wonder if the flat was haunted.

WYSIWYG, Tim repeated to himself for the rest of the day. What you see in daylight is all there is, he was sure. All the same, things had changed. Every time his mind was in neutral, it was not Big Danny who filled his thoughts now but that bundle of clothes in the night. What if Rox was right? What if his room was haunted? Ridiculous, he'd never heard anything stupider. He decided that tonight, in the interests of science, he would refuse to sleep. That way his WYSIWYG theory would be proved.

Later that night he lay rigid in his soft, familiar bed and counted all the knobs on the fancy snowflake in the middle of his ceiling five times. He would not close his eyes. Six times he counted the knobs. Seven . . . *the crowd was calling Tim from the reserve bench to save Man U from certain defeat, when his heart started bumping.* . . .

Tim jerked awake. In the far corner of the room by the window, he could just see long, skinny fingers, wiping and smoothing each other in the half-light. There was no body. Against Tim's better judgement, every hair on his body stood on end.

"Who's that?" he whispered.

The hands placed their palms together, the leathery fingertips upwards.

Tim's heart was crashing now but he refused to let his terror get the best of him.

"Don't you dare disappear," Tim called. "I want a word with you."

If Tim closed his eyes for a split second, he knew he would regret it. He tried not to blink but his eyes began to tickle. If he counted 1, 2, 3, 4, 5, 6, 7, – he could hold off that blink – 8, 9, 10, 11, 12, 13 . . . he must keep counting – 20, 21, 22 . . . His eyes were burning into his brain.

When it finally came, the blink felt warm, moist and utterly glorious. Tim opened his eyes again. He was dazzled. A candle flame was inches from his nose. He quickly shut his eyes and saw the flame turn green inside his lids before he opened them again.

23

Behind the flame Tim could see nothing but darkness so deep that he could only imagine a face. It felt close to his own, as a horrible voice stretched out a long, grating whisper, "Laaaaard."

"Go away, you nasty old nightmare," Tim yelled. "Leave me alone."

This wasn't real. It couldn't be. WYSIWYG.

Mum suddenly appeared at the bedroom door.

"Mum, it's horrible," Tim moaned.

"But Rox is in bed, love."

"Not her. Can't you hear it?"

"What, darling? What?"

"I think he's saying Lord or Lard or something. And he's got a candle."

When Mum said, "Who has?" Tim gripped her tighter than he'd ever held anything in his life.

They scrutinised the bed, the floor and Tim himself. They even looked under the bed but there was nothing there.

Roxanne arrived next, rubbing her eyes and sat on the bed, "This is getting beyond a joke, isn't it? Scary voices, weird dreams and bumps in the night."

Mum told her to be sensible and get back to bed.

"But you know what's happening here. Don't you?"

"Don't be silly, Roxanne, Tim's just having some rather lively dreams."

"But aren't you frightened, Tim? With a real ghost in your room? Are you going to sleep with Mum and Dad?"

Tim felt like crying. Instead he hissed, "There's no ghost. That's a stupid idea!"

Rox went off to her room and came back with her fist clenched.

"If your dream person keeps calling for the Lord this might help," she said, handing him a big, silver gilt cross.

Tim slid it under his pillow with a muttered thanks. He felt foolish enough without Rox and Mum making it worse so he sent them both away. He checked the bed again and jumped in. There was no way he could sleep though. No way . . . *the crowd erupts as world-famous striker Tim Exworth approaches the goal mouth to make a cross. Yes, he's done it — it's a useful cross* . . .

Chapter Five

Rox came down to breakfast the next day dangling one of Georgie's trainers.

"This," she said with her face scrunched up in disgust, "was in *my* room."

Georgie stuck out his tongue at her and shouted, "What do you call a ghost who plays football?"

"A ghoulie!" said Tim, as Rox stuck out her foot under the table and a kicking match started.

"Children!" Mum shouted. "Cut it out."

"But Mum, Georgie's always creeping around my stuff."

"Have my room instead," Tim offered sweetly, flipping the cross into the air. Last night's nightmare wasn't bothering him anymore. "Perfect for witchcraft. Excellent aura. Ancient curses a speciality."

The cross clattered to the floor.

Tim had an idea. At last Rox would get the fright she'd deserved for years.

"Ro-ox! The ghost cast a spell on my teeth in the night. Look!"

He pulled his eyes apart and grinned his house-of-horror face, exposing the cross sideways in his mouth where his teeth should have been.

Rox's eyes went wide. A scream burst from her mouth and shot up to the very top of the flat where it threatened to strip off the new wallpaper.

Tim removed the cross from his mouth, "I take it you don't want to swap then."

"TIM!" shouted Mum, as Georgie cracked up laughing.

*   *   *

That afternoon Mum took Georgie shopping. Tim and Rox were supposed to be revising for the start of term tests. *No way on the last day of the holidays*, Tim thought. He was busy with something much more urgent. He was creating a new database on the laptop, called WYSIWYG. He would gather all the information he could find on matters supernatural into the one file. On one side of the page he would put all the scientific evidence against and on the other side there would be a slim column for the spooky, speculative rubbish. The imagined stuff. If any. But a true scientist must not rush to conclusions. A true scientist would gather all available evidence and examine it calmly. Without interference from sisters. Or dreams. His research would start in the software encyclopaedia.

Rox opened the door and snooped over his shoulder.

"Try *phantom*," she said. "With a p-h."

"No matches found for phantom."

"Or what about spectre? Try spectre. Hang on a minute, this could be close – *spectroscopy*. What's that?"

"Studying spectra."

"What's a spectra?" Rox asked.

"More than one spectrum," Tim said smugly, " and a spectrum is a range of something. Let me see it. Yep, there, '*an arrangement in order of magnitude of radiated frequencies of electromagnetic waves.*'"

"What are electromagnetic waves? Is that like when you wiggle all over the place on your skateboard?"

Tim looked at his sister waving her arms like a mad aeroplane. He could have explained speed wobble to her. He could have explained that his skateboard had turned up, yes, but that his spare glasses weren't all that had gone missing. He still couldn't find his skate tool. He could have told her that the skate tool is a special spanner for tightening up the trucks and tight trucks mean no more speed wobble. But he couldn't be bothered. Instead he read out,

"*They are oscillating electric and magnetic fields travelling together through space at speeds of nearly 300 million metres per second.*"

"Oscillating." She was enjoying the word.

"Waving about," Tim said.

"Cool. What do they look like?" Rox asked, looking out the window. "Can you see them in daylight?"

Tim cleared his throat, "You can't see them. But they can be measured . . ."

She broke in, "You can't see them? Don't I remember you saying, correct me if I'm wrong, but didn't you say that if you don't see it in the daylight when you're awake, it doesn't exist? What You See Is What You

Get? Are you telling me, *as a scientist*, that there's something out there that we can't actually see?"

Tim's teeth felt superglued inside his head. He was cornered – by his own theory.

* * *

That night Mum sat on Tim's bed and read to him. She hadn't read to him at bedtime for years but she'd announced that Tim was looking peaky and needed help to get to sleep. In fact, as an actress, Mum's idea of bedtime reading involved so much dressing-up and quirky voices that sometimes everybody was up laughing until after midnight. Tonight though she was trying to be soothing. She'd chosen one of Grandpa's favourite books and the familiar words drifted over Tim like a breeze: *"as the Mole looked, he lived; and still, as he lived, he wondered . . ."*

Mum snapped the book shut.

"We all wonder, don't we darling, but ghosts," she said, reminding him sharply why she was busy being soothing in the first place, "ghosts, of course they're nothing but imagination."

"No way." It was Rox in the doorway, "Deirdre Johnson has a ghost child who plays their piano every full moon and Alex's dad says that sometimes a woman comes into his bed."

"Rox!" Mum stopped her sharply, "could you just get ready for bed."

"But . . ."

"Now!" Mum hissed and Rox finally left.

Tim wished Mum would go as well but she kept hanging around.

"Girls getting hysterical over nothing," she was saying. "You could always come and sleep on the camp bed with Dad and me if you really . . . "

"No thanks," Tim said. "Honestly you can go now. I'll be fine."

Rox was back, "What's that shadow there? Look! It's moving!"

Tim looked behind him – at nothing.

"Got you!" Rox was jeering as she scratched her nose with a stick before running off.

That stick. Tim felt outrage seeping through his veins. Rox had not been scratching her nose with a stick at all. She was scratching her nose with a bone. One of *his* dinosaur bones! She *had* stolen them. And he would get them back from her if it killed him.

* * *

Next morning, Rox marched confidently ahead of Tim as they crossed the road on the way to school. Tim was wondering why their first proper day back was always a Tuesday and why couldn't they have every Monday off? Tuesdays off would be good too, especially today.

His eyes were prickling with lack of sleep as he shuffled down the hill, stamping on one or two dead leaves and checking through his list of worries. The growth rate of that list made it nearly creepy enough to feature in the WYSIWYG database in its own right.

Top of the list, as always, was what were his chances of a whole day without trouble from Big Danny.

He hadn't even made it through the gate when Big Danny jostled him from behind. "Got your skateboard moving yet, Timmy Wimmy?" he sneered. "With you on it, I mean!"

He ripped Tim's bag off his shoulder and threw it to Pitbull Pete who threw it back to Danny.

"Oy!" Tim shouted. "You'll crush up my lunch!"

"We'll crush up his lunch, will we? Wanna crush up Timmy Wimmy's lunch?" they whooped to each other. The bag flew from one big boy to another and Tim flitted between them like piggy in the middle. Everybody was laughing. The sound throbbed in Tim's ears, as he rushed from one wet jeering mouth to the next. He was waiting for them to kick out or hit him.

The bell went. The bag landed in a nearby garden and Big Danny and Pete ran into school.

"I'll get you!" Tim bellowed, as he climbed over the garden wall into the road.

Hold on, did he really say that? Was he mad? Luckily they'd all gone into school and couldn't have heard.

Chapter Six

Big Danny ignored Tim for the rest of the day but those three words kept looping around in Tim's mind — I'll get you! He could only hope that they weren't rolling around inside Danny's tiny brain too.

He fell into bed that night and pulled the duvet over his head. The only way to forget Big Danny was to go through his other worries. He squeezed his eyes. Now all he could think about was Rox in *his* room with *his* dinosaur bones the night before. How was he going to get revenge? He could think of something brilliant if only he wasn't so tired.

I need sleep, he thought, *the nice, plain, dreamless sort* as he drifted off.

He sat up, eyes wide open. He could have sworn he heard a whimper. A disembodied finger advanced slowly through the darkness.

"You don't frighten me," Tim lied. He picked his nose and reached out his own slimy finger until it nearly touched the other one, point-to-point. The misty finger shrank back. Tim had a sensation of sand sprinkling down his spine. He tried to ignore it.

"Look," he said, "I don't want to sound rude but I'm tired and I want some sleep." Suddenly it occurred to him that here was a situation where a clever person could solve two problems at once.

He addressed the finger, "Assuming for the moment that you are a ghost, which incidentally I do not believe, I've got this . . . person I know," he said, "called Danny. You'd love him, and he'd love to have a ghost. I know he would. I'll give you his address"

No answer. Nothing.

Tim thought for a moment, "What about Rox's room then?"

Tim could feel a shudder in the air. He laughed out loud and wasn't afraid anymore.

"Rox too messy for you, is she?" Tim asked. "Okay. Would you go away if I found you somewhere tidy to haunt? The tidiest place in the whole world?"

Tim jumped up and landed painfully on a marble on the floor, "Follow me."

As he led the way down the circular stone staircase, Tim's bare feet froze more with each step. He had lost all feeling in both big toes by the time he stood at the shelf in the hall. There was Dad's railway season ticket parallel with the edge of the shelf. There was his change, in two pyramids beside the wallet. Tim opened the smooth brown leather – plastic cards on one side, smooth new notes on the other. Under a sheet of clear plastic was a photograph of Mum from years ago with long, dark hair, before even Rox was born.

"Here you are! The tidiest place in the world. My Dad's wallet."

A wail rattled the windows.

"Ssssh. You'll wake everybody up. Let me get some sleep and I'll think of something else."

Silence.

Then a voice hit Tim with all the agony of the world.

"LARD . . . LAaaard, Laaarrrddd."

Tim pulled Rox's crucifix out from under his pyjama top and held it up as if he was in some dodgy horror film. "Why do you keep calling for the Lord?"

"No, lard," rasped the voice. "White grease. I need it for my hands. They're so dry and hard."

Tim thought this was the stupidest dream ever. He went back to bed and hid under his duvet again. Only three more days of school to get through until the weekend.

*   *   *

"How I love the smell of black pudding in the morning," Dad said, dropping a lump of butter in a frying pan and watching it melt and turn brown at the edges. "Want some, Tim? It'll stoke you up for football. Hasn't this week gone fast?"

No, Tim thought. Why did grown-ups always say that? The first week back at school always felt like a century, even when you weren't lying awake every night worrying what you were going to dream next.

"Tim!" Dad called. "Wake up, old man."

Tim lifted his head up from the table.

"How about a few sausages too," Dad asked, "and a bit of fried bread?"

Before Tim could say yes, Mum looked up from her new script. She'd got her first real acting job for months.

"Not so fast, my beloved fatso!" Mum said, as she struggled from her chair. "You were twelve stone when we married and you'd better be twelve stone again soon or you'll crack these old floorboards."

"I love it when you're rude," Dad said, gripping his frying pan hard, "it brings out your dimples."

"Cooking them in *lard*, Tony. Of all things." She was looking genuinely cross.

Tim looked up, "Is that lard?"

"Butter," Dad protested, but Mum didn't care.

"You'd better tidy up. That MacFadyen man is due again at ten."

"On a Saturday! Why can't he snoop round his own home?"

Mum forced open Dad's fingers, took the frying pan and tipped the slimy chunks of black pudding into the bin. "Muesli, Tony," she smiled.

"Why's Mr MacFadyen coming back? Tim asked.

"He's checking up on us again in case we've thrown something ancient away. I bet he lives in a caravan with a roof as bald as his head," Mum said.

"Don't be rude to him, darling," Dad said. "We need him on our side."

"I won't even speak to him."

"You will," Dad replied.

But Mum wouldn't budge, "I can't, I've got these lines to learn and then I've got to finish Rox's cake."

Tim felt a stab of worry, "So who's taking me to football practice? I've got all this kit to carry. I need help."

Mum and Dad looked at each other. Then they spoke together, "Gran."

*   *   *

After all the noise and steam of the family kitchen, Gran's flat was peaceful, pink and smelt of soap. On a shining white plate she laid two slices of buttered toast and cut them into triangles.

"You ever want feeding up, you just come straight down here, love. That's what Grannies are for. Would you like honey on them? Or marmalade? Why not have both?"

"Thanks, Gran." Sausages would be nice too and chips and sauce but he didn't want to push his luck.

Gran sat opposite with her cup of tea and stared at the table. She'd been doing a lot of that lately. She turned the spoon over in her saucer and looked as if she was going to say something. Tim just kept eating.

"I'd be happy to take you to football," she said. "A run in the car would do me good."

There was silence again.

Gran chewed on her false teeth and muttered to herself, "Lord help us."

"Have you got any?" Tim asked.

"What, love?"

"Lard."

Gran didn't think to ask why, she just opened the fridge, took out some hard white grease and cut him a piece the size of a school rubber. Tim stared at it briefly before he wrapped it in a piece of kitchen paper. Then, all too aware that this time he was wide awake, he told Gran he'd be ready to go in a minute and took it back home.

He raced upstairs.

"Go on then," he told his empty bedroom. "Lard."

He wasn't sure whether he felt like a scientist or just stupid as he unwrapped the paper and laid it on his duvet.

Tim's whole body shivered, as the lard rose slowly off the bed, squashed itself flat and disappeared. It had been there and now it wasn't. Tim was frantically patting the bed to make sure it was gone when a crackling sigh filled the air.

Tim ran.

* * *

Well, he had to. As soon as he got back from football, he sat down and entered the experience in the spooky column of the WYSIWYG database. By the time he had written it all out, the column contained a worrying amount of information. Several pages. He leant back in his chair wondering what he might balance it with on the other side, when he became aware of Rox's presence.

"Where's my book?" she demanded from the doorway, "my *Horrendous Hamper of Horrible Ghost Stories*?"

"Get back. You're not allowed in here, even if it is your birthday and give me back my dinosaur bones."

"Do you a swap?"

"Show me the bones first."

Rox disappeared. A minute later she was at the door again, pretending to comb her hair with the bones.

"Can't even take a joke," she moaned.

Tim let it pass. He reached under his pillow and slid the ghost stories book along the floorboards to Rox's feet.

"They're useless," he said, "those stories. Ghosts aren't like that."

"Ghosts are all in the mind," Rox replied, "Didn't you say so yourself? WYSIWYG: What you see is what you get. That's what *we* scientists say."

Rox dumped the bones on his desk.

Tim ignored her. He pressed Ctrl Alt on the keyboard. He pressed again. That was odd.

"What do *you* scientists say about this then?" he asked. "The WYSIWYG file has disappeared."

"Spoo-kee," Rox cooed. She lurched over and bashed Ctrl Alt sixteen times and the Enter button and ten or so other buttons before declaring the whole laptop totally useless.

"No, it's not," Tim said, "just this one file." Again and again the screen pulsed with the same message: 'WYSIWYG FILE – ACCESS DENIED.'

Rox pulled her hair onto the top of her head, trying to look intelligent.

"The ghost's taken it."

Tim definitely wasn't telling her about the lump of lard.

"Rox," Mum called from the kitchen.

"A ghost has *not* taken it," Tim was seething, "of all the brain-free, ridiculous things I ever . . . "

"Rox!" Mum called even louder. "What colour do you want the icing on this birthday cake?"

Rox stuck out her tongu
clever, I've got more brains in m

Tim cut in, "than you've got in y

Rox was half-way out of the door
to Tim.

"If only you'd admit it — just once — th
right."

"If it ever happens," Tim snarled, "I might."

Seven

"You think you're so
little finger . . . "
your whole head!"
when she turned
I could be

appearance of the
ied rather than say
d happened to her
to add one or two
im was out skate-
...ed from talking to
...s. but it kept disappearing. In chunks.
Then some of it would come back and disappear again. Terrifying. To interfere with the laptop meant Warfare with Tim with a capital W. Thank goodness it had happened to him too.

But today of all days she had other things on her mind. As soon as she walked into lunch everybody sang Happy Birthday. Grinning, Rox opened her last birthday card and shook the envelope. There just might be money in it. She took out a letter and stopped smiling.

Mum, seeing her reaction, grabbed the letter and read out the apple green scrawl, *"To all at Flat 1, God and Goddess read my verse."*

"Somebody knows how to treat neighbours with proper respect then," Dad said.

Mum read on,

"God and goddess read my verse, mojo magic wills this curse to send the evil back on he who wish me harm. So mote it be.

Your neighbour, Fuschia Baldock."

Rox broke the silence, "Don't think much of her syntax."

"Don't be cheeky, young lady," Dad said, "somebody has upset our new neighbour. Any ideas? Rox? Tim?"

They shook their heads, silently remembering the old lady's weird capers on the day of the eclipse. Georgie's chair scraped as he tried to escape.

"Georgie?" Mum asked.

Dad met his eye. "Georgie did I see you playing round Mrs Baldock's washing?" he asked.

"It was an army of knights, Dad."

"He didn't do any harm," Mum said. "He was using his light sabre, for goodness sake."

Georgie sprayed his mouthful of birthday cake in protest, "The washing was all grimy anyway, Dad."

"I'm sure it was, son. What that woman wears under her combats does not bear thinking about."

"I didn't mean to knock it all on the grass," Georgie shouted. "It just happened."

Mum rubbed her face with both hands. Georgie was acting up because he missed their old home so much. It was the last thing she needed right now.

"Look," she said, "if there's anybody else you're planning to offend, can you just tell me now? It's bad enough that MacFadyen man prowling around this morning, without this!"

Georgie's nostrils flared with rage, "I didn't mean it!"

41

"Well, you'll have to apologise, Georgie, we can't have her hexing us."

Georgie yelled, "No way," and ran for it.

* * *

"A fine start this is with a new neighbour," Mum said as she and Rox reached Mrs Baldock's front door.

"A fine start this is to my thirteenth birthday," Rox muttered. She should have been getting ready for her birthday sleepover that night.

Mum spread one arm in the sunlight and thumped her chest, "Battle and lust of blood Move ONWARD!"

"I don't see how quoting lines from your play's going to help," Rox mumbled.

Mum pulled the black iron loop by the thick wooden door and a jangle sounded inside. She called through the letterbox, "Anybody in? It's the Exworths."

There was shuffling inside.

"Mrs Baldock? Hello?" Mum called again.

Chains jangled and the door opened three inches. A mouse looked out, nestling in grey human hair, above a slice of wrinkled human eye. Above the hair Rox wouldn't have been a bit surprised to see a witch's pointed hat, but she didn't.

"Mrs Baldock," Mum began, "about your note . . ."

"Wh-what a lovely mouse, Mrs Baldock," Rox stammered, glad she was at least two metres away from the four-legged little darling.

"Hear that, Henry? Girl thinks you're lovely. Don't tickle, Henry," she said to another mouse on her shoulder. A third peeped out of her shirt pocket.

Mum was trying to get a word in, ". . . I'd just like to say . . ." when Rox asked, "What's that one called?", pointing at number three.

"Henry," was the answer. "And all I want to hear from you lot is sorry."

Before they could speak again, the door clacked shut. A cloud slid over the sun and Rox and Mum shivered.

"Is there no SUN to light, No thunder in heaven, NONE to SMITE such INFAMY?" Mum hurled the words at the door.

Rox knew better than to come between Mum and her new role.

Mum rang the doorbell twice more, to silence, and they turned for home. "We'll have to write back to her. If she has eight mice, do you think one's called Henry the Eighth?" Rox asked.

"There's a tradition, you know," Mum said, " that if you're having a party and you're expecting it to be noisy, you invite the neighbours."

"No way! She's not coming to the sleepover! We'll all be as quiet as Henrys. I promise."

They barged back into the kitchen.

Dad was amazed to see them back so soon, and was even more amazed that Mrs Baldock had resisted Mum's charm. He had another solution.

"TO WHOM IT MAY CONCERN," Dad scribbled on a large, brown envelope. His other hand was under the desk hiding a bar of chocolate.

"Who's coming to tear our lovely home to pieces now, darling, or is it Rox's crowd already?" he asked, as the doorbell rang.

43

"It's Jack — the plumber." Mum smiled. Tall, handsome, eighteen-year-old, ponytailed Jack walked in and said his first job was to cut off the water supply.

"No washing?" Mum shrieked.

"No baths!" Georgie and Tim cheered.

"No loo!" Dad moaned.

"How can I have my friends to sleepover with no loo?" Rox asked.

"We'll use Gran's," was the answer.

Rox gazed at Jack as he parked his bottom by the sink and answered his mobile. Rox found herself staring at a pale tattoo of a serpent on his forearm. She looked up, and found him smiling at her.

"He's just your type," Tim was whispering in her ear, "being a male. Feel like a party for two? Just you and Jack?"

Rox had to get out of there quick, before everybody noticed she was blushing.

"Shut up, you idiot," she whispered back and grabbed Georgie by the hand. Since the first mention of having no loo, Georgie had been wriggling oddly. The last thing Rox needed was Georgie causing trouble at her sleepover.

"Georgie," she said, holding on as he tried to run away, "let me show you the way to Gran's loo. Just so you know, okay?' Besides Gran hadn't given Rox a birthday present yet and Rox felt it was time for a little nudge.

*　*　*

44

There was no need. As soon as Georgie had used Gran's bathroom, she settled him in her kitchen with paper and felt tip pens and said to Rox, "I've got something I want to give you, dear."

Rox watched her lift a blue velvet jewellery box down from the top of her wardrobe. Music tinkled as it opened.

"Your grandfather gave me this box when we got married. I don't know how he managed to afford it. Nobody had any money at all in those days. When I die, this jewellery box will be yours."

"That'll be lovely, Gran, but you hold on to it for a nice long time. I'd rather have you alive."

"Oh, I don't want to live too long, love."

Gran gazed at herself in her three dressing table mirrors for so long Rox wondered if she was counting her wrinkles.

"But today is a special day, isn't it?" Gran said, finally. "First day of your teens. Happy Birthday, love. This is for you."

Gran pressed a necklace of black beads with a silver clasp into her hands.

Rox could hardly speak, "Gran, it's beautiful."

Gran fastened the clasp behind Rox's neck and let the beads fall in a sparkling black tassel at her throat.

"They're French jet. He gave them to me on our fifth wedding anniversary. Worth quite a bit now probably."

"Gran, I can't . . ."

"You enjoy them, love. They suit you. And don't you let young Georgie get hold of them . . . talking of which we'd better see what's he up to."

Georgie was busy colouring in bold strokes of orange, pink and black.

"What is it, dear?" Gran asked. "The Universe?"

Georgie just tutted and kept going, "It's Mrs Baldock."

Rox pressed her lips together to keep in a laugh. Georgie always got very angry if anybody was rude about his art.

"What's that on her head?" she asked. "Like sparklers? Is it a head-dress?"

Georgie reached for another pen. "No," he said. "It's her hair."

"And how many arms has she got?"

"Seven," Georgie explained, "for the dancing."

"Lovely, darling," Gran purred, "can I put it on my wall?"

"No," Georgie said grimly. "I need it. I've got a plan."

"Well, it'll have to keep," Rox said. She'd just caught sight of the time. "I've got to go, Jess and Alice will be here any minute."

She kissed Gran and raced home, leaving Georgie slaving away over his portrait.

Jess and Alice were already in the hall, talking to her mum when she rushed in.

"Sorry," Rox panted. "I was at Gran's."

The three friends flew up to Rox's room and soon tuneless chanting was oozing from Rox's new CD player through the smoke of a joss stick. The girls sat cross-legged on the floor and every fingernail and toenail in the room had been painted black. Their throats were sore with laughing, but now the lights were low. They were engaged in the serious business of the evening – ghosts.

"Then," Rox whispered, "it began to disappear very slowly from the outside in."

The door creaked opened and a voice shattered the atmosphere.

"Jess a song at twili-i-i-ight, when the lights are lo-ow!"

"Dad, you promised, no singing."

"And the flick'ring shadow-ow-ows softly come and go-ho."

"Go *away*."

Rox squeezed the door shut and began again.

"So," she whispered, "all he could see, hanging in the air, were those awful wringing hands and all he could hear were the distant words, Lard, lard . . . "

"Rubbish," said Alice. "That's the worst ghost story I've ever heard. Ghosts don't go on like that. Listen I've got one. And this really, really happened."

Chapter Eight

Alice squeezed her throat a bit to make her voice rasp and her eyes went wide.

"It was a moonlit night," she croaked, "and everybody was fast asleep, except," — her face went deadly serious — "for the three friends who were staying in the abbey overnight for a dare. They didn't believe in ghosts. Oh no. They were hugging each other tight because they liked each other so much."

The three girls hugged each other tight.

"They were shivering," Alice went on, "because it was cold."

They all shivered dramatically.

"Suddenly from the chapel came . . . the unmistakable sound of moaning and . . . a clanking of chains."

Rox clamped her hands over her ears, "No!"

"Yes," Alice hissed. Her eyes looked as big as boiled eggs. "Suddenly something dropped to the floor with a horrible squelchy sound and the ghost shouted, 'Oops, I've dropped my head!'"

They all started giggling so hard their faces nearly burst and they barely heard a floorboard creak in the corridor outside their room.

"Sssh," Rox tried to sound serious but she couldn't stop laughing, "what was that?"

The girls held their noses to keep the giggles in. It couldn't last. They were soon rolling around on the mattress, stuffing their sleeves in their mouths. Rox called through the door, "Who's that?"

The floorboard creaked again.

"It's only wee me, Meery Queen of Scots," squeaked Jess.

"It's the banshee of Ould Connemara come to claim our souls," Alice boomed.

"Our souls!" Jess shrieked, as though it was the funniest thing she had ever heard in her life.

Rox inched open the door, looked out and shut it again.

"Out there," she said, "is the most terrifying thing I have ever seen in my life!"

She knew who was in the corridor, and that it was somebody alive and not a bit frightening, but Alice and Jess didn't. They both stopped giggling. As if on cue a wail came from the other side of the door, a long ghostly, "WOOOOOooooo!"

"Help!" Jess squeaked.

"Don't open the door," Alice whispered.

"I will so," Rox said, "are you ready? You don't want to miss this."

Rox swung open the door, "It's . . . Banshee O'Georgie!"

Georgie stood in the corridor draped in his bed-sheet. Instead of cutting holes for his eyes (he'd never dare) he had the sheet draped over his head. As he waved his arms around, the girls could see his green, spotty pyjamas underneath.

"What's this, Georgie?" Rox asked, pulling at the sheet's elastic edge and making it balloon like a dress. "You look more like Cinderella than a ghost."

Alice and Jess were shrieking and covering their faces, pretending to be really spooked. Georgie poked his head out of the sheet.

"Leave off," he wailed. "I'm the ghost of Greenwich Abbeeeey – back from the dead to annoy you."

"Well, you've got that right," Rox said, "you've never been more annoying. Go away!"

Mum suddenly appeared from nowhere and gathered him up.

"Bed, young man," she said. "Don't let these big girls bully you."

"He started it!" Rox said.

"We ALL must suffer; do not weep TOO much," Mum warbled, going into her role again, and whisked him away.

"Where were we?" Rox sighed and closed the door.

"I know," Alice laughed, and pulled her eyes long again, '"Oooops, I've dropped my head . . . '"

*   *   *

At eleven o'clock Mum came back to turn off the music, so the boys could sleep. Rox protested, it was a party after all and tomorrow was Sunday, so they were granted fifteen minutes more.

Mum stomped away crowing, "Even the birds of the AIR tend with affECTionate care the PARENTS to whom they owe their birth And living."

"Why does your mother go on like that?" Alice asked.

"She's an actress," Rox murmured.

There was a moment's silence.

"I wish I'd a Gran like yours though," Alice went on, "those black beads are fantastic."

"They're French jet."

"Real jet?"

"I think so. Why?"

"Well," Alice said, crossing her arms, "my mum's acupuncturist says jet protects you against ghosts."

All three fell silent.

A sound came from the corridor. It was as blood-curdling a sound as the girls hoped they would never hear again. It was the sort of sound you might make if you'd run out of tennis balls and were bashing clumps of blood-soaked bandages against a wall.

Rox stood up, pulled down her sweatshirt and strode across to open the door.

In the landing stood a headless monster in grey school trousers. Rox tugged its white cotton polo neck down sharply and uncovered Tim's head.

Tim grinned a grin to fry the bone marrow of the most fearsome sister on the planet and repeated the sound, a magnificent burp.

"Excuse me," he said and raised a hand to his mouth. From the end of his sleeve, where his hand should have been, a huge bundle of dinosaur bones poked out like the flaky hand of a decayed corpse.

Rox couldn't help it. She shrieked.

"Now who can't take a joke," Tim said.

Rox growled, "Shove off or I'll kill you!" and slammed the door.

"First Dad, then Georgie. Now him!"

Alice laughed. "When's it Jack's turn? Is that what he's called, that gorgeous 'boyfriend' of yours?"

"If only," Rox said. "There's only one place we're going to get any peace round here. Follow me."

Rox knew she was supposed to stay away from the balcony off her bedroom. Nobody knew yet whether it was safe or not but she was dying to show it off. The lock was stiff at first but eventually the French doors creaked and with a final push, the cold night air rushed in. They stood staring at a glittering vista of London's skyscrapers beyond dark ancient trees.

The girls crept outside, whispering and rubbing their arms. They could see their own breath go misty for the first time that autumn. An almost full moon beamed from behind the Abbey tower, veiled by a skein of cloud.

"Aaooowww!" Alice howled like a wolf. It was irresistible. Jess and Rox howled too, louder and louder.

Jess held out the edges of her jumper like a skirt and began to dance. "Romeo, Romeo, wherefore art thou, Romeo?"

They ran to and fro, to the edge of the balcony and in again, to and fro. Rox danced too, brushing against the black iron railings crusted with paint until she could see the rockery and lawn below.

It was when she danced alongside the railings again that she felt it.

"Don't," she said.

Something pulled her again, closer to the edge and she heard that voice again, *'Admit It!'*

"Look, *STOP IT*!" Rox shouted. "The railings will collapse."

Jess and Alice stood still.

"Stop what?" Jess said, barely outside the French doors.

Alice stepped back inside the bedroom. "I'm going in," she said, "if you're going to be crabby. Anyway, it's freezing."

They both turned to go back inside.

"I'm not being crabby, it's just . . ."

"What then?" Alice asked.

"Something pulled me. Something tried to pull me over the railings," Rox said.

Jess couldn't see anything.

"Me neither," Alice said. "Have to be pretty strong to pull you, Rox."

"Well if you're going to be . . ." Rox stopped. What was the point? She was shivering so much she could hardly speak. She badly needed to go inside and get warm.

As she crossed to the bed Rox collided with her mum who had hurtled in to see what all the commotion was about.

"Too much cola," Mum declared, as she closed the French doors. "I thought somebody was being murdered! That balcony is off limits!"

Rox tried to explain, "But Mum . . . "

"And too many silly stories if you ask me," Mum went on. "As quiet as Henrys, remember? Now get some sleep!"

How could Rox sleep? Alice kept snuffling in her ear and on the other side, Jess was lying on her back, her breath flapping in and out through half-open lips.

Rox closed her eyes. Like a comforting hug, Dad's voice sang inside her head: "As the flick'ring shado-o-o-ows softly come and go-ho-ho-ho-ho-ho-ho-ho-ho-ho-ho"

That laugh . . . on and on it went. It wasn't like Dad's laugh anymore. A man's voice, yes, but with an edge, a bitterness, almost a taunt in it.

"*Stop it,*" Rox shouted in her dream, "*stop it! Don't laugh at me, I hate it!*"

The laughing stopped.

Then she wished it hadn't.

A voice was scorching through her sleeping bones like a stream full of loathing and streaked with spit,

'That jet has let you fret
and sweat within the net
I set for you.
But jet, like coal all wet,
in silver set,
that jet can't set you free . . .'

"*Go away!*" Rox begged the nightmare voice. She clenched herself tight against the horror. "*GO AWAY!*" she shouted in the dream, as she felt something tugging her arm.

Chapter Nine

"Rox?" a voice whispered.

Rox looked over the top of her duvet at a head poking round the door. It was a dear, familiar head with two floppy ears and no nose. Rox nearly wept as she reached for him – "Lamby!" – and started to hug him.

Georgie was still attached.

"Geddoff!" he whispered.

Rox apologised, keeping her voice down so she didn't wake up Alice and Jess.

"I'm just . . . *very* pleased to see you. Both of you," she whispered.

Georgie was looking grim.

"Do you want me to take you to Gran's loo?" Rox asked.

Georgie shook his head and tugged her along the corridor to their own loo.

"Look," he muttered, pushing the frosted window open.

Rox leant outside, "What?"

"I don't like her," Georgie whispered. "She makes me feel funny."

"Who?" Rox hadn't a clue what he was on about.

"You know who," he whispered. "She was dancing again. With no . . ." His voice trailed away in embarrassment.

Rox crouched down so that their faces were the same height. "Mrs Baldock?" she said, "with no?"

Georgie nodded.

Rox was trembling again, and not just with cold. Could Mrs Baldock have had anything to do with what had just happened on her balcony? She pulled Georgie close and hugged him. He was shivering too. As she closed the window, he said, "Can I tell you now?"

"What?"

"My plan. I want to do my plan."

They tiptoed to his bedroom where he proudly showed her his picture of Mrs Baldock. He was right to be proud. It was now clearly the back view of a woman as wide as a sofa, with several waving arms, dainty dancing feet and a hairdo made of giant sparklers. She had not a stitch on.

"It's going to be a spell," he spat angrily. "Mojo magic back at her!"

"You little gem," Rox laughed. "Wait a sec."

She scampered to the bathroom and came back with nail scissors.

"A lock of my hair," she snipped, "and some of yours." Snip. "Some of Lamby's too for luck." Snip.

"Fingernails?" Georgie asked, spreading his hands. Snip. Snip.

"What else?" Rox asked. "We need the spell itself. What'll it be?"

Georgie stood stiff like a soldier and said, "Mrs Baldock, witchy woo, we have had enough of you."

"Perfect." Rox wrote it on the back of the picture. She took up the rhyme, "Stop the dancing and get dressed, You're old enough to know that's best."

Georgie laughed and took his turn, "Your behind's as big as half the Abbey. No, twice as big! And twice as flabby!"

Rox dropped the pen, she was giggling so much. This was exactly what she needed after her fright on the balcony. Good old Georgie. He was annoying sometimes but she loved him a lot. Georgie felt under his bed and pulled out one of Dad's envelopes. On it, in Dad's writing, were the words, TO WHOM IT MAY CONCERN. Georgie fed the picture with its rhyme into the envelope and sprinkled in the hair and clippings. He was sealing the flap and patting it when Rox put her hand over it, suddenly serious.

"What are you doing?"

"Got to give it to her".

"We can't," Rox insisted.

Georgie was not in the mood to listen. He pushed the sealed envelope back under his bed.

"I can. First thing in the morning," he said.

Rox sat on Georgie's bed, suddenly overcome by exhaustion. What a night. Whatever happened, Georgie's envelope must not reach Mrs Baldock. There was no way she'd see it as a joke. But Rox hadn't the energy to argue about it now. She could just about manage to tuck Georgie into his bed and feel her way in the dark back to her own bed. She was hoping with every fearful breath that she'd be able to get some sleep.

* * *

It felt like an earthquake but it was only Alice bouncing up and down on the mattress. Rox had slept after all.

"Everybody up," Alice shouted.

"Why?" Jess groaned, on Rox's other side, "it's only half-eleven."

"I'm starving," Alice announced, "come on, where's breakfast?"

A letter in green ink lay on the kitchen table.

"It's for you girls this time," Mum pointed, as she took skimmed milk from the fridge and poured a tiny splash into her peppermint tea.

Rox felt a stab of fear. Mrs Baldock was the only person she knew who wrote in green ink. Had Georgie gone and delivered his spell already? She read out the letter:

"To Flat 1,

Wicca herbs and magick flowers,

Fill you all with magick powers;

May the holder of this charm,

Be freed from HOWLING, pain and harm."

"You see," Mum said, slicing a grapefruit ferociously, "you should have asked her to your party."

Rox read on:

"You keep your pets from howling at night or I'll call the police. No idle threat.

Your neighbour, Fuschia Baldock."

There was no mention of Georgie's picture, thank goodness. Alice and Jess were trying to swallow their giggles but Rox was furious.

"Cheek! She's the one dancing around with nothing on. Have you got that in your letter, Dad? Dad!"

Dad hadn't had a chance to deliver his reply to Mrs Baldock's first note yet and was merrily running up some threats of his own as a PS. He covered it up as Mum turned around.

"Your mother's taken it. I know you have," he growled.

"Taken what?" Mum asked.

"My envelope. On the top here. It was marked TO WHOM IT MAY CONCERN and everything."

"What's wrong with this one?" Mum asked, holding out another envelope.

"It's not *the* one. But it'll have to do."

Mum put on her glasses and read from the nineteenth page, *"Or we'll sue you for slander, libel, rudeness AND for having no clothes on, you nasty old bat.* Tony! You can't say that."

"Why not? It's what she is."

"What's got into you? You're usually so polite. With strangers, I mean."

"Lack of saturated fats is making me tetchy. In the Tetchy Olympics I could be Mad Tetch from Tetch Hard III. All I need's a cooked breakfast, then I'd even love Mrs Baldock to bits."

"Okay," said Mum. "You can have one sausage."

While the girls were packing for home, and Dad was launching into two fried eggs, mushrooms, tomatoes, toast and one grilled sausage, Georgie tiptoed down the stairs. He was sneaking through the hall hoping to avoid company of any kind and in particular the company of his mother. He nearly fell over in horror at the sight of a large sealed envelope propped on Dad's desk. Could it be his envelope with his spell? Had Rox told everybody about last night? How could she?

Glancing left and right, Georgie squeezed Dad's envelope up his jumper, scuttled outside and put it in the bin.

On his way back he stopped behind the door. He could hear voices in the kitchen.

"But what about the hands pulling me off the balcony?" Rox was asking. "Twice!" Jess said.

"You said it was once." That was Tim. "Well?"

"Well what?" Rox asked.

"Was it once or twice?"

"Twice." Rox's voice was unsure.

"What did you feel *exactly*?" Tim asked.

"Don't fluster me!" Rox bawled at him.

"We need to know. For the WYSI . . ."

"I don't know!" Rox was nearly in tears, "just leave me alone."

"I'm glad I haven't got a brother," Jess muttered, as she and Alice tried to comfort Rox.

Leaving her alone was the last thing Tim had in mind. She was doing it again, taking centre stage, casting everyone else in shadow. But she did seem genuinely embarrassed and afraid, a sensation Tim was finding surprisingly enjoyable. If she *had* felt something, he needed to know. The WYSIWYG file was still missing, so he had opened WYSIWYG 2. This time he was not going to bother listing scientific facts.

He had enough on his hands keeping up with the uncertainties. He couldn't get the disappearing lard out of his mind. At least he hadn't told Rox about it. Otherwise there'd be no stopping her. It was bad enough having to face the idea that, however remote the possibility, Rox just might have had a genuine supernatural experience.

"So it's imagination then?" Tim said. "Nothing but dreams?"

"If I was going to dream about somebody touching me in the night, I wouldn't dream it was like that, would I?" Rox asked.

"You'd dream about the gorgeous Jack." That was Alice.

Rox glared at her, then rounded on Tim. "All your ghost did," she shouted, "was hold a candle and shout lard and you were crying like a baby. I'm talking about attempted murder!"

"She's right," Jess said, to avert violence, "she *was* shouting at us."

"She usually does," Tim muttered.

Georgie nodded behind the door.

"SHUT UP!" Rox shouted, and they all started laughing.

"I *felt* it," Rox was fighting down tears now. "I *did*!"

Tim had to cough he was laughing so much. This was Rox alright — she'd do anything to make sure she was the centre of the action, including making up the action itself.

"We've been over all this before," he said, "WYSIWYG." He wasn't going to even think about seeing the lard on his bed squashed flat.

"What?" Jess asked.

"It stands for What You See Is What You Get," Tim explained, "that everything has a scientific . . . "

"But I thought *we* scientists," Rox interrupted, "admitted there *were* things we can't see. Waves and stuff."

"And love," Mum chipped in. "Now much as I love you all, it's time we were going. Your parents are expecting you home. And this argument could go on all day."

Georgie scuttled outside just before Mum shooed all the girls out to the car. "One last thing to do before we go," Mum said. "I've got to deliver your father's polite note to Mrs Baldock. I won't be long."

Mum hunted in the desk, the boot cupboard, even in that drawer in the kitchen full of bits of string and old pencil sharpeners. She had nearly given up when, who would have thought it, the envelope turned up under Georgie's bed.

"I've had about enough of his behaviour," she muttered, as she locked up and walked down the path towards Mrs Baldock's front door.

Rox was applying new blueberry lip-gloss at the car mirror when she saw Mum behind her, skipping up Mrs Baldock's stone steps.

Uh-oh, she thought as the envelope disappeared into Mrs Baldock's letterbox. She wasn't sure why but she had a terrible feeling that if Georgie's spell hadn't reached Mrs Baldock earlier, it had now.

Chapter Ten

Tim stood in front of the hall mirror with both his eyes tight shut. He was engaged in an experiment for the WYSIWYG 2 database. He was trying to see what he looked like when he was asleep. Eyes open: awake. Eyes shut: what? Asleep? Awake? Could be either. He had to admit it — there were times when what you see is what you get, and other times when it might not be.

He opened his eyes. In the mirror he saw a figure drift behind him towards the stairs. It was Rox, back from delivering everybody home. She had a towel over her head under which Tim could see black sunglasses.

"Where do you think you're going, young lady?" Dad called from the kitchen.

"Back to bed."

"No you don't. Somebody's got to get Georgie's envelope back from Mrs Baldock's."

Rox had had to tell. Things would only get worse if she didn't, but she wasn't pleased with herself and wanted to be on her own. She wafted silently on up the stairs.

"Mum'll go, won't you, darling?" Dad asked.

Mum flapped a hand. She was up to her eyes in e-mails.

"Gran, you're not busy, are you?"

"Well, it is 2.30, you know Tony. Time I went down for my five heaped tablespoons of *All Bran*. Desmond always had his five heaped tablespoons of *All Bran* at 2.30." And Gran legged it too.

Tim knew what was coming next.

"Tim? TIM?"

Tim put his glasses on again. He'd keep very still behind the pillar, well out of sight.

Georgie, dressed as a pirate, had tied Lamby to the banisters and was giving him twenty lashes.

"Georgie, where's Tim got to?" Dad asked, coming out of the kitchen. "He was here a minute ago."

Tim stared at Georgie and put his finger to his lips.

"Dunno," Georgie said and lifted his eye patch to stare back at Tim.

"It'll have to be you then. It's your spell after all."

"I can't," Georgie said. "She's bigger than me."

"She's bigger than all of us," Dad said seriously.

Tim pressed flat against the wall. He could feel a sneeze rising.

"Why can't you go, Dad?" asked Georgie. "I said I was sorry."

"I'm too scared."

In the silence of their shared recognition of Mrs Baldock's ferocity, Tim's sneeze got the better of him.

Three minutes later, he stood on Mrs Baldock's doorstep wondering why he had ever been born. His hand quivered as he reached for the black bell pull. There was still time to run away. It was Sunday. Maybe Mrs Baldock was out at a Black Mass or something.

She wasn't. The door opened and six eyes glared at him, two belonging to Mrs Baldock and four belonging to a couple of mice sitting in her hair.

Only Mrs Baldock spoke, "So-o-o-o — you've come to say sorry for the rumpus, have you?"

"Er . . . "

"Come in." Before he could say no Tim had been yanked in by his collar and was standing on the mat in her hall. The place smelt of old ladies' perfume, polish and mice. Behind his ears he heard scratching. Could it be one of her mice? Actually on his head?

The door thumped shut and a dusty brown curtain swayed over it.

Mrs Baldock growled again, "So what *have* you come for?"

Tim felt goose pimples run up his back in a sudden draught. The curtain fluttered as if somebody might be behind it. A picture of a pink ballet dancer seemed to be giving him a funny look. With more than a little alarm Tim realised that Mrs Baldock was coming closer to him and that she was going to touch him. He could smell burnt toast off her.

"Yes," she said, as she put her hands flat on his head.

"I think I better go now," Tim mumbled.

She ran her fingertips over his eyes, nose and chin.

"Yes, Henry, this is a special boy — a psychic boy. You've come on behalf of your Grandma, haven't you?"

"Er . . . "

Mrs Baldock's fingers were moving through his hair right down to the back of his neck. Or was it tiny paws? She threw her head back hissing, "I have a message for your Grandma." A very deep baritone voice suddenly shouted from Mrs Baldock's mouth:

"In the wardrobe facing west
Is a drawer on the left.
There are collars labelled best
And silken ties of warp and weft
Beneath the undies washed on Mondays,
There's a gift for YOU!"

Mrs Baldock dipped her head again, sighed and pulled at her combats.

"I need the loo," she said in her usual voice and bumbled off down the hall.

"Weird!" Tim said to himself, as he scratched his hair with both hands. Next minute he saw a long, brown, ribbed, hairless mouse tail dangle in front of his eyes. Now he did like mice but a decision had to be made and he made it. He knocked the mouse off his head. It landed on its back, righted itself and scuttled up the curtains.

Was that whispering behind him? Tim whipped round and saw no-one. He turned to the front door. The dancer in the picture was giving him another funny look. Then he saw it. How had he missed it before? On the telephone table beside a knobbly, old typewriter was a large envelope marked TO WHOM IT MAY CONCERN.

The loo flushed lengthily at the end of the corridor. Mrs Baldock was waddling towards him. Time was running out.

Tim stuffed the envelope under his fleece. For what felt like ages he fought with the clammy brown curtain and finally pulled the latch aside. He hauled the door open and ran up the path to Gran's front door.

He heard Mrs Baldock, calling, "Come back here," as he held his finger on Gran's doorbell. He looked behind to see if she was after him. No sign of her, yet. No sign of Gran either. As he wheezed in panic, Tim found himself wondering how you catch your breath. Maybe in a balloon, like the way they'd measured their lung capacity in science the other day. It must be the stress.

At last – Gran was coming to the door.

"Who's that?" she called.

"Me, Gran. Tim. Let me in. Quick."

"Kim?"

"No, Tim. Your grandson," he pronounced carefully through the letterbox and heard her twist two keys, unlock three bolts and – it was taking ages – unhook a jangling chain.

"What's with all the locks, Gran?" he said, falling into her hall at last. "Do you think *they're* coming to get you or something?"

"Who are? That Kim, whoever she is? Or is Kim a man? I knew a Major Kim in the war. Big chap, with bad feet."

"There's no Kim. Nobody's coming, as far as I know. Well, she might be. Mrs Baldock, I mean."

Gran poured him some squash.

"You're the image of your Grandpa when you frown like that," she smiled.

Tim told her what had happened.

"So what's this rhyme then, eh?" she asked.

Tim had been racking his brains but he could no more remember it than he could catch his breath in his own fingers.

"In the cupboard facing east," he started, "sorry Gran, it's gone."

"Well, while you're trying, you can help me. I can't find my *All Bran*."

Tim knew how she felt. He still couldn't find his skate tool or his spare glasses. But he could manage with one pair of specs. For Gran to lose her *All Bran* was disaster. Gran's day was not complete without *All Bran*. She got herself all of a dither, as she called it. Tim laid the rescued envelope on Gran's sideboard and jostled his memory,

"In the cupboard in the east,
You will find her morning feast.
Under the undies washed on Mondays . . ."

"AHA!" Gran shouted from her larder. "Did you say undies? What have we got here, under my basket full of undies ready for the wash tomorrow? Well, well. I've never known a rhyme find my *All Bran* before. Not in all my born days. Useful person, this Mrs Baldock. I think I'll have a word with her."

Poor Gran, Tim thought. She really was starting to lose it if she was keeping her cereal in the laundry basket. He would mention it to Mum.

Chapter Eleven

School was almost peaceful after the weekend's turbulence. It would be even better if he could keep distance between himself and Big Danny. So, for the whole of first break Tim stayed in with Mrs Cox and tidied up.

"You are a kind boy, Tim," she said and gave him more coloured pencils to sharpen. "What a very helpful boy you are."

Tim's skateboard was safe at home but they'd taken his lunch box again that morning. He knew what would happen when he opened it. Wet crumbs would fall all over his trousers because his drink would have leaked into everything. His sandwiches would be mush balls with his *Kit Kat* crumbled to brown powder. The worst of it was being hungry all day. And every lunch-time there was Big Danny looking at him across the classroom, laughing and whispering, "Eat it up now, Timmy Wimmy. Every bit."

Every time Tim heard the words 'Big Danny', or heard somebody rumbling behind him on a skateboard, he wanted very, very much to punch somebody. So when the bell rang after lunch and they were all turned outside to play, Tim did the only sensible thing he could think of. He hid in the loos.

He sat for what seemed like half his life, listening to other boys come in, do their business and go out again. Listening time after time made Tim want to do the same but he didn't dare even put his feet on the floor. He just sat, both feet up on the wall, feeling the edges of the silver cross in his pocket. He'd started carrying it after the ghost took the lard. Not that he was telling Rox that he hoped it might have supernatural powers but he wished with all his heart that it had. Then it might be some help against the likes of Big Danny.

There was the bell. One more minute would make him late for class but by then Big Danny should be safely in his seat.

"He's in here, Dan. Look, it's locked but there's no feet showing. Can I break it down?"

Tim groaned — Pitbull Pete.

Big Danny trod — slop, slop — along the sticky floor.

"No. No need. We'll just ask him nicely and he'll come out like a lamb. Won't you, Timmy Wimmy?" Danny growled. "You better if you know what's good for you."

For years Tim would remember the fall of his stomach as he drew the latch back and let the door flop inward. For years he would remember Big Danny's broad, grinning face.

"You see? He's a reasonable little tyke really. Arntcha, Timmy Wimmy?"

Big Danny grabbed Tim's hair and pulled him down to the wet floor. Tim knew all too well what it smelt of but had never thought to examine it so closely before. A punch on his back flattened him onto the tiles. He kicked out as he felt somebody untie his lace and take off his left shoe.

70

"Nice trainers!" Danny jeered.

"They're not trainers. They're skate shoes!" Tim said.

"Trainers! Trainers!" they sang, as Tim got to his feet fast and hopped from Danny to Pete trying to grab his skate shoe. It was piggy in the middle all over again except that every time one of them caught the shoe, they whacked Tim on the head with it before they threw it on. Tim's head bulged with pain at every blow but he would not cry.

His glasses wobbled and hit the floor. Danny's left boot was hovering over them when Mrs Cox's voice cut through them all, "So! Not only are you *not* in class where you're supposed to be, but *fighting*!"

Danny dropped the shoe and Tim knelt to tie it on again. He was hoping that if he kept small and quiet she wouldn't see him. It was no good.

She folded her baggy arms. "Tim Exworth too. I'm shocked. And disappointed. What have you got to say for yourself?"

Tim felt his chin wobble.

"Well?" she said.

Tim knew it was not really a question. He formulated a long sentence in his mind featuring the words 'not' and 'fair'. Big Danny cleared his throat behind him suddenly, like a gunshot, and Tim knew there was no point.

"Nothing," he said.

"Right detention for all of you," Mrs Cox said, shooing them back to the classroom.

*   *   *

Tim examined the teeth marks on his yellow pencil. He could hear whoops and laughs outside as everybody else went home. Everybody except Big Danny, Pitbull Pete and him. Seven words were chalked in capital letters on the board: 'WHY WE SHOULD NOT FIGHT AT SCHOOL'.

What could Tim possibly write? That you have to fight because if you don't, everybody thinks they can have a go at you? That he wasn't fighting in the first place, he was being picked on? He turned round to look out the window and got the fright of his life. Big Danny was making an eel-sucking face at him. Tim swung back to his paper and decided to just write anything he could think of.

'We should not fight at school because the teachers don't like it,' he started. *'Neither do I. What I like best is my skateboard but I can't ollie yet. An ollie is a jump where it looks as if the board is stuck to your feet. It's not really stuck but you can make it look that way if you hit the tail with your back foot and drag the side of your front foot along the board as you go up. I like football too.'* And he listed the best school First Eleven team he could think of, described his favourite tricks and strategies and then wrote *'Morale! You can't punch it or kick it or trip it up but in football it's the most valuable . . .'*

Mrs Cox tapped her pen on her desk, "Okay. You can go now."

Typical. Just when he was beginning to enjoy himself. *If I finish this sentence and this paragraph and this page*, he thought, *with luck Danny and Pete will be safely on the bus home by the time I leave.*

The plan worked but it wasn't until Tim let himself into the abbey's vaulted hall and breathed in the delicious cooking smells of home that he could relax. Then he remembered. He was probably in for more trouble for being in detention. The only person he could see was Rox perched against the kitchen table, apparently talking to herself.

"So your father's a criminal?" she was asking. Tim dumped his school bag on the table and made for the biscuit tin. This was probably not the time to ask Rox why she was wearing eye make-up on a school day. There was a pouring sound and a short swear word. Jack the plumber was busy on something intricate under the kitchen sink.

"Mmm. He's in prison, in the Scrubs," he finally mumbled.

"That's fascinating. What did he do?"

Jack's hand felt in his wide navy bag for a hammer.

"Made big money. A millimetre too big."

"Ha ha. Very good," Rox simpered, as Jack's pony-tail disappeared under the sink again.

Tim mimed putting two fingers down his throat, bit into a stack of chocolate digestives and wandered back into the hall.

As Tim walked up the stairs, Rox called up to him, "Mum wants you!"

That was all he needed.

"You do know," Rox went on, "she's been up the walls and down again about you fighting."

Tim hadn't time to say anything before he collided with his mum on the landing, blowing her nose into a tissue.

"I'm appalled, I really am," she sniffed.

So was Tim, by the callous lack of justice at his school, especially in Mrs Cox. Tim longed to tell her everything. He needed her to help him and a start would be getting him some spare glasses. Big Danny was getting obsessed by them and he'd nearly crushed them today. But as usual the wrong words came out.

"I got detention."

"I know that!" she shouted. "What I want to know is why?"

Tim looked down at his trainers.

"Because . . . " he said slowly.

"Fighting!" Mum cut in, "fighting who? Is he hurt, the other boy, is that why you got detention?"

This was too much. Nobody was giving him a chance, even at home. He pressed his nose and sniffed.

To his alarm Mum sniffed too. He looked up and saw tears waiting to roll from her eyes.

"Mum?"

"It's just . . . there's Georgie getting up to all sorts, and you, and now your Gran." Her tears fell. "She's been in there *all day* with that Baldock woman. They phoned me twice to ask for more wine but I told them all the off-licences were shut.

She gave a long sigh. "You can hear them laughing from here. Listen. If that Baldock woman *is* a witch, I don't know what I'll do. Your Gran's so vulnerable at the moment."

Tim hadn't had a chance to tell Mum how Gran stored her cereal these days. It didn't matter. Mum had obviously got the point on her own. Gran wasn't anything like her normal self these days.

His mum pinched the bridge of her nose and announced, "We've got no choice."

"What do you mean, Mum?"

The tissue was a ball of tiny shreds as she spoke, "We'll have to go and save her."

Chapter Twelve

Tim and his mum ran across the lawn. She picked up a handful of gravel, threw it at Mrs Baldock's front door and rushed behind a bush. Tim quickly dived behind a tree in case Mrs Baldock came out and blamed him. There was no response, so Mum did it again. Tim was amazed. Gran wasn't the only one losing it.

The front door opened a crack and then flew wide open. Gran stood on the doorstep swaying slightly. She shook Mrs Baldock solemnly by the hand.

"Thank you, dear f'wudderful time!" Gran shouted, as she tottered to her own flat.

"Mum? Are you all right?" Mum called. Blanking her completely, Gran undid all the locks on her front door and went inside.

"Tim," Mum ordered, "Go and find out what they've been up to."

"Why me?"

"Will you do what you're told, for once!"

"I've still got all my homework to do."

"Go on, you're good with your Gran."

Tim walked to Gran's front door with dread.

Mum shouted, "And we've still got your detention to talk about. I haven't forgotten, you know."

The perfect end to a perfect day, Tim thought sourly, as he rang Gran's bell.

She must have been just inside because the door sprang open.

"Fine woman, Mrs Baldock," Gran said, as she and Tim walked into the flat. "Full of insight."

Tim's mouth fell open, not just at these words but at the sight of Gran's bedroom. Gran's rooms were always neat with lacy squares under pots and lamps. Today her bedroom was a shambles.

"She believes in reincarnation, you know. Having another life as something else after this one . . . "

"I know what reincarnation means."

". . . she has done since she was a caterpillar," Gran went on.

She straightened and drew a five-point star in the air over the empty drawer. "She read my hand."

"Why, what did you write on it?"

"No, she read the lines. Lifeline and so on. At first I was so tense she was reading my fist. But once we got going, it was brilliant. She had candles."

"And mice?"

"And mice. One's pregnant. They're like that, mice. She got me to fill in a form and where it said Sign ·Here, she wrote Aries! Ha, ha. It was the best fun I've had in years."

She sat on the bed and fingered Grandpa's green jersey.

"He's all right, you know. He misses me and everything but he's fine," she smiled. "Now where was I?"

Gran got up, fetched a needle from her basket and dangled it over the jersey. "Right, Tim. Where's west?"

He pointed west.

She started chanting,

"In the wardrobe facing west,
Is a drawer on the left,
There are collars labelled best,
And silken ties of warp an . . ."

". . . weft. Gran! You know it! What is weft any-way? Is it like in the bible, Jesus weft?"

Gran smiled again. This could become a habit for her.

"No," she said, "it's when you're weaving cloth, the warp strands go one way and the weft go across and through them. But it's no help. Your Grandpa didn't have silken ties of warp and weft. I'll keep looking though. You never know."

Tim looked at himself in the mirror above Gran's bedroom sink. He nearly said out loud that it felt, it really did, as if there was somebody else with them in the room. As if he might sit up in bed any minute and say hello, Grandpa's last toothbrush and razor were still in Gran's tooth mug.

Tim had been hoping he could persuade Gran to explain to Mum about his detention, get her to understand. Gran had helped him out before. But it didn't look as though she was going to be much use today. She dropped the needle and began poking under the bed.

Tim swung open the door of Grandpa's wardrobe. He had only looked inside it once before, when he was about four and Gran and Grandpa were getting ready to go to the ballet. Grandpa had blown both his cheeks out like a hamster to make Tim laugh. Tim could still visualise him standing there in front of the drawers with their printed labels: Handkerchiefs. Gloves. Collars.

"Mrs B's a ballet fan, you know," Gran said, as she sat on the bed. "Your Grandpa loved ballet. We met at *Swan Lake*. I'd been sick in the interval and Desmond took me the next night again in case I was put off ballet for ever."

"What was it like?"

"Hard to say really. I was sick again. But I knew that very night that Desmond and I would be man and wife."

Gran unbunched a pair of Grandpa's socks as she talked. "It's done me a power of good to talk about him, you know. I wish your mother would. But she won't. All she does is fuss — fuss, fuss, fuss."

Tim knew what she meant but thought it best not to say. Instead he tugged at a drawer labelled Collars. The whole thing fell out and landed by his toe. Gran came over to have a look.

"Well, bless my soul. I never thought I'd see that again." She bent to pick up a roll of dingy tissue and opened it as if it were made of fairies' wings. "Desmond," she whispered, "of all the places to hide it."

Gran placed the tissue and its contents reverently in Tim's palm and said, "There. That's for you love. He was terrific at it, you know, a real star. And now it's yours."

It looked like a baby robot's thigh bone. The tissue almost collapsed as Tim peeled it back some more and saw that the worn holes must once have been six-sided.

"He wants you to have it," Gran said. "I know he does. Grandpa's best ever ice-skating spanner."

"Thanks Gran," Tim said and glanced at Gran's wedding photo on her bedside table. She and Grandpa were both laughing, maybe at the fact that he still had hair. Grandpa couldn't hug her properly because his arm was in a sling as he'd broken his elbow on the skating rink the week before.

Tim had never really liked ice-skating. Mum's threats about people slicing your fingers off if you fell had put him right off. But he held Grandpa's spanner in his pocket as he mooched back to his own kitchen.

Mum was pacing round going "Where's your father when I need him?" when the front door banged. Dad was home.

"Mmm, smells great," he said as he entered the 'Inquisition Chamber', "what's thawing?"

Mum exploded in fury about how nobody understood how ghastly everything was for her, Gran was going bonkers and to cap it all Tim had been in detention. She turned on Tim, "Why the detention then? What was the fight about? Well?"

"But all the best people get detention," Dad said. "I was always in detention at school. Wasn't that how I got to be such a brilliant accountant. I mean they're going to name a loophole after me!"

Suddenly Dad's face puckered. Mum took one look at him and took his hand and kissed it.

"So brilliant an accountant, you'll be running the whole firm soon," she said, "don't you worry."

Dad mustered a smile and hugged Tim with his free arm.

Tim couldn't believe it. Was he off the hook? He opened his mouth to speak. Wouldn't it be great if he could explain to them both about Big Danny and how the detention hadn't been Tim's fault and how he hated all this?

But it was too late. Dad was back in the hall with Mum smoothing his hair while he emptied his pockets. He was talking to her too quietly for Tim to hear. What about me, he wanted to shout. Why don't you listen to me?

*   *   *

After dinner Tim followed Dad and Mr Architecture Expert MacFadyen on a tour of the flat. The three of them stood on the landing looking at the horizon where six trailers lay in a circle on Blackheath. The trailers were hung with coloured signs in the evening light.

"Autumn fair this weekend," Mr MacFadyen sniffed. "Means it'll rain. Nothing surer." He tapped his clipboard, "Back to work."

They were counting windows.

The phone rang. It was one of the work piggies for Dad, so Mum swooped from the kitchen to the hall and shook Mr MacFadyen's hand as though she was pumping him.

He looked a bit afraid.

"Mr MacFadyen," she said. "WHAT an unexpected pleasure."

"Ever the actress," Rox murmured. She put her plate in the dishwasher and ran for cover in her room. Mum and Mr MacFadyen were coming through to the kitchen.

"And in here ONE WINDOW!" Mum announced.

"One," Mr MacFadyen repeated, ticking his clipboard.

Tim had given up trying to talk to Dad on his own, so he'd started his homework in the dining room.

"And in here ONE WINDOW," Mum said again.

Mr MacFadyen ticked again, mumbling, "One."

"Haven't you counted me before?" Tim asked.

"No, darling, it's the windows. Mr MacFadyen is of the opinion that we own twenty-*four* windows and your father's notes say twenty-*three*. We're in pursuit of the missing window, aren't we, Mr MacFadyen? What an interesting job you do, Mr MacFadyen. As if I hadn't got other things on my mind . . ." she murmured, as she swept from the room.

Mr MacFadyen trotted after her, clutching his clipboard, looking nervous.

"Mrs Exworth, these details matter, you know. You don't want to throw my calculations out, now do you?"

"Big mistake!" Tim muttered.

"Mr MacFadyen," Mum spun on him like a whirlwind. "Throwing your calculations out is what I would dearly love to do. And this window — do you agree

82

there is just the one window in this hallway? – this window will do nicely."

She reached for his clipboard.

Tim ran out of the dining room to have a look. His mum was trying to unlock the hall window.

Mr MacFadyen was begging, "Mrs Exworth, there's no need for a scene now, is there? Mrs Exworth! Mr Exworth!"

Chapter Thirteen

Tim watched Mr MacFadyen and his clipboard running away down the gravel before Dad closed the front door.

"Your mother shouldn't let that man bully her like that," Dad laughed. *Dad*, Tim thought, *can we have a talk about bullies?* But before Tim could say anything Dad had scooped up the seven-year-old pirate captain.

"Come on, Georgie, bedtime," he said. On the way up the stairs he played on Georgie's toes: "This little piggy went to the office.

This little piggy stayed at home.

This little piggy got black pudding,

And this little piggy got none.

And THIS little piggy went ahh, ahh, ahh just like Mr MacFayden."

Tim mooched into the kitchen.

"You're quiet, Tim," Mum said as she hung up the tea-towel. "Why don't we go up to the chapel and you can give me a hand?"

So now Mum wanted a chat. That usually meant her asking lots of questions and him thinking of ways not to answer them. Tim would rather have talked to Dad about Big Danny really. Dad was better at listening.

Mum's plans for the chapel included a big bath with feet and bulby taps and a mirror all along one wall. She'd said so with great excitement on their first visit.

"And I'll lie here up to my neck in bubbles drinking champagne," she'd laughed, "thinking of things for all of you to do."

But as Tim followed her up the stairs she said nothing. Apart from her attempted assault on Mr MacFadyen, she had been less than herself lately. She was like a football with a slow puncture. An e-mail had come at the weekend that she'd said couldn't have mattered less. Tim had the idea it might have something to do with her weird mood.

"I don't know how the bathroom will work out in here," she whispered. "It's a bit small really but it's got fantastic atmosphere."

As Tim closed the door and heard a shivery clack sound zig-zag along the tiled floor, he wasn't so sure. The air felt thicker in here than anywhere else, as if it was full of invisible cobwebs.

Mum's hands lay softly on Tim's shoulders as he turned on the light, "Now tell me, love . . ."

Here it comes, Tim thought.

" . . . is Big Danny leaving you alone these days?"

"Sort of."

"What do you mean, sort of?" Mum searched his face. "Is somebody else being horrible to you? Is that why you were fighting? What is it? You can tell me, you know."

Tim looked anywhere but back at her.

"Do you want me to see your teacher?" she asked. "Would that help?"

As if.

She sighed from the pit of her stomach. "Is it this place then?" she asked.

Tim shook his head.

"Do you want to go back to our other house?"

Tim shrugged. If he said yes, it would make no difference. He looked down at his skate shoes. Mum put one of Grandpa's old shirts over her clothes and opened some sample pots of paint.

"Mum," he mumbled. She didn't hear.

"It's all turning out so . . . " she began, waving her brush, " . . . so complicated."

Tim pulled out Grandpa's spanner and started fiddling with it as Mum started slopping seven different shades of yellow in patches all over the walls.

"It's so dark in here with all these gloomy tiles, what it needs is sunshine. But all this paint's more like dog sick. What do you think?"

Without giving him time to answer she went on, "It's not just that everything's costing so much but my acting job's gone. Did I tell you? That e-mail at the weekend," she sighed. "I learnt all those lines for *Electra* for nothing. I might as well have been planning my celebration speech for winning the Oscars. You were right I should have been an ice-skater."

Now Mum was being even odder than Gran. Tim had said nothing about her being an ice-skater. He'd never been asked and frankly if she brought a skateboard or skates anywhere near his park, he'd emigrate.

Her arms flowed out from her sides like wings. "Remember what you used to say when I was four,"

86

she laughed and poked Tim's chest, "don't be afraid to stick it out."

Tim became aware that he was hovering on the edge of a conversation that did not include him at all.

"What are you talking about Mum?" he asked.

"Your bottom. Stick it out when you skate. It's all balance, so weight forward. Oh and one other thing — don't give up."

Her fists clamped to her temples, "Oh Daddy, I did try, I tried so hard!"

This was embarrassing. Tim started to tip-toe to the door. Before he could open it, Mum wiped her hands down the shirt and said, "What's that in your hand Tim? Show me."

He held out the spanner. Mum took it and cradled it in her palms as if it were made of diamonds.

"Oh God, I remember this. Did your Gran give it to you? How wonderful. I'm amazed she kept it."

"Well," Tim started to say, "she didn't really know . . . "

"He used it to tighten up his skates, so the blades wouldn't wobble."

"Speed wobble," Tim muttered to himself. "Grandpa knew about speed wobble!"

Mum clasped the spanner to her chest.

"He was brilliant on the ice, you know. Balance, he used to say. It's all speed and balance. He'd such a peculiar action. He tried to teach me but I never got it right. It was like this," she laughed, as she stuck her bottom out again and tried to slither backwards with a lop-sided smile. Her smile dropped suddenly.

"Try pretending to listen at least Tim," she said.

"I *am* listening."

"Then stop that ghastly noise."

Tim wasn't aware of making a noise. "What noise?"

"That scratching, on and on."

She hunched her shoulders and pressed her fists hard against her forehead to hold back tears.

Tim was dazed with embarrassment. He knew that Rox would have had no trouble putting her arms round her mother and going, there, there. She wouldn't even have to be sincere. What does there, there mean anyway? But what could Tim do? He tried to reach out to her but his arms would not go higher than about forty degrees. He was preparing to say, I know, Mum, I miss Grandpa too, every day. I miss him so much that I feel he's with me sometimes. Maybe I'm imagining it. I must be but I can smell him and I think I hear him sometimes just behind me out of sight.

Tim raised his arms again. No problem this time, he was ready to hug his mother and do his best to comfort her. He stepped towards her.

"I told you, stop it!" she snarled.

Tim felt hurt pinch his heart.

"Stop what?" he stuttered.

"That horrible scratching. You're driving me mad."

With tears streaking her face, she thrust Grandpa's spanner into his hand and stamped out of the room.

Tim stared after her. He felt as if she'd just ripped him in half. How could she walk away like that? His arms flopped. And what scratching? He had heard no scratching. This place was driving them all insane.

He was suddenly aware of a scent, hardly there but he knew it immediately, a smell of warm, woolly jerseys.

"Grandpa?" he said. "Are you there, Grandpa?" There was no answer, but Tim didn't need one. He knew the answer was yes.

But Grandpa couldn't be the ghost – could he?

Chapter Fourteen

Rox was jubilant. Not only had she made it through a whole week without ghostly visitations but victory was hers and it was sweeter than jelly babies under the duvet at midnight. Tim had got a letter that morning from the Natural History Museum. She had caught him opening it as she arrived in the kitchen.

"Up at the crack of noon as usual," Dad said.

"It's Saturday," she pouted.

"We're going to hear about Tim's bones," Mum said, before a row started. "Well? Are they Jurassic or what?"

"No," Tim swallowed. "They're twentieth-century fox bones."

"I knew it!" Rox shouted. "I was right."

She, Rox, had been right. She, Rox, had a duty to make him admit it several times that day just for starters. The bones were exactly what they looked like, disgusting old rubbish. What You See Is What You Get.

Tim was not taking his defeat gracefully. When Rox asked if he was coming to the fair with her and Georgie, he'd replied that he'd rather be tortured by aliens. Besides he had football practice.

Rox made a sour face.

"Come on, Tim, I've got to look after Georgie. Which means I'll be stuck on the baby rides. If you come, I can leave the two of you together and do something death-defying."

Tim shrugged. She'd know all about death-defying if she had to do football practice with Big Danny. He was probably sharpening his studs with a special outsize pencil sharpener at that very moment. If Big Danny inherited a skate tool, it would be the right size instead of being used up years ago. And Danny's would work with one firm twist. But Tim said none of that. He just went off to football.

*   *   *

Drizzle hung in the air as Roxanne and Georgie crunched along the path.

"What's it going to be first, the Thomas the Tank or a donkey ride?" Rox asked.

Georgie narrowed his eyes at her. He still hadn't forgiven her for telling everybody about his spell. "The ghost train first, then the dodgems. And I'm driving."

"Your feet don't . . . "

"They do so!" Georgie cut in. "Then I'm going on the big hammers that swing you upside down and all the grown-ups lose all their wallets in the grass."

"You'll be sick."

"I don't care."

Mrs Baldock's front door opened and the old woman walked towards them. Georgie's bravado evaporated. He hid behind Rox.

"I just want to give you this, dear. Your Gran told me it was your birthday. It's a book I had when I was a girl. I've felt strange things coming from you lately . . . "

Rox and Georgie were backing off towards the gate.

91

"Come back here!" Mrs Baldock bawled. "I'm talking to you."

Rox shuffled back, with Georgie still hiding behind her.

Mrs. Baldock started again, "I just thought you could do with cheering up."

"Thanks Mrs Baldock," Rox said, surprised. "Odd things have been happening."

"Just to you or all over your flat?" Mrs Baldock asked.

"All over," Rox said. "Nothing special. I don't know, noises and stuff." She suddenly remembered the howling and started going red. "Em . . . I don't mean the howling, that was just us having a laugh. Er . . . sorry if we woke you."

"Thought so," Mrs Baldock said and bit on her pipe. "Never mind that. It's these other noises. I think there's something you've done, you know. To awaken it."

Georgie peered from behind Rox, "Us?"

"Awaken what?" Rox asked but Mrs Baldock just went back inside.

Georgie shuddered. "She still gives me the creeps. Wake up what?" he asked.

"Don't ask me," Rox said. "Forget it, we've got serious fun coming up." She took his hand, "Come on! The quickest way to the fair is through Greenwich Park."

The rows of chestnut trees looked huge in the mist, larger than life, as they walked along. Georgie kicked up damp drifts of leaves, as Rox opened the old book.

"For Fuschia from her loving Godmother Alice, 1934," she read out. "*The Winsome Twosome* by

Edwina Heythrop-Hawkins. Chapter 1. 'Once upon a time there was a happy ending.'"

"Short book," Georgie muttered. He heard steps behind them, as if somebody was walking on his heels. He turned to look but there was no-one there.

"It's not like the rest of the pages are blank, stupid. 'The Happy Ending led a rather dull existence until it encountered Neville and Dorothy . . .'"

"Boring," Georgie said. He heard another footfall behind him. He took Rox's hand, "Come on, Rox, I can see the hammers! Let's run."

At first it was the smells that excited them most: smells of diesel, hamburgers and the distant presence of the Blackheath donkeys. But as they ran together to the Ghost Train and a painted skull stared down at them with a spider crawling out of one blood-red eye socket, they both knew why they were there.

"Don't you go frightening my ghosts in there," the man said, smiling as he took their money.

"His ponytail's a bit like Jack's," Rox whispered as they climbed onto the cracked leather seats. "Except Jack's is longer and shinier and it's not grey."

Georgie ignored her.

Their heads fell back as the car crashed through black swing doors into the darkness.

As they clattered out again, Rox was jabbering, "It's okay, it's not frightening. We're fine."

Georgie knew that. He didn't need Rox to tell him that the witch hooting over their heads was a tape or that the cobwebs trailing over their faces were just string. He couldn't wait to go round again. By himself. It was going to be brilliant.

"You have to wait right here for me after the ride," Rox said, as she went off to get them some candy floss.

"Okay," he agreed, as his car crashed back through the swing doors again.

Georgie's ghost car burst through to fresh air a second time. As his car chugged to a halt, every hair on his head urged him to get out. He wanted to run, as fast as he could, a long way away without looking back. But he stayed. And he looked. Of course he looked. There sitting beside him in the car, her face as pale as Edam cheese, was Mrs Baldock. Her mouth opened wide like a slash but her eyes were not smiling. They glinted at Georgie, holding him dazed in his seat.

Georgie managed to wrench his head round, saw Rox and ran to her.

* * *

"But why are we following Mrs Baldock?" he whinged. "I don't like it. Somebody was behind us on the way here, do you think it was her?"

Rox stopped and held both his hands.

"This rain's horrible," she said. "Aren't we ready for home anyway?"

"We've just got here," Georgie said. "I don't want to go yet." But he was lying. It was pouring now but there was something else. It made him long to be in his bedroom with his mum cooking something delicious that would be ready any minute.

Rox had something else on her mind. The old woman looked like a head-case, but she was the one person Rox could consult about spells. A love spell — that might work on Jack. She'd suddenly had the idea on the way over. She pulled Georgie along.

"Mrs Baldock," Rox shouted. "Wait for us!" They caught up with her as they walked through the park gates. "Gran says you're a bit of an expert in certain matters," Rox panted.

"She's a stupid old twit, your gran," Mrs Baldock growled.

"Excuse me?" Rox said, looking confused. They fell behind again as the old woman raced up the road.

"I thought she was Gran's friend," Georgie whispered.

"Me too," Rox whispered back, "this isn't like her at all." But Rox was still determined to pick the old woman's brains. "Mrs Baldock!" Rox called. "Gran says you do spells — is that true?"

Mrs Baldock grunted, "Maybe."

"I was wondering — do you do love spells?"

The old woman's laugh rang high in the trees, a scary laugh that cut through them both like wire. They stepped back. It wasn't like an old woman's laugh at all.

"What sort would that be? One to make somebody fall in love with you?" Mrs Baldock smirked.

Rox kicked a stone casually across the path. "Um, yeah."

"That's the usual sort," the old woman cackled.

They walked on.

Georgie broke the silence.

"Rox?" he asked, "Are you in love?"

"Don't be so daft," she snarled, "and I'll kill you if you say anything about this to Mum. Or Dad . . . or Tim."

"Well?" Rox asked. "Can you help me?"

Mrs Baldock paused. Scanning the ancient trees, dark and thick like the legs of giants hiding in the storm clouds, she said:

"Get heart of a dove, liver of a sparrow, womb of a swallow, kidney of hare. Crush to a fine powder. Add your own blood and put the love powder in the food or drink of the one you love and whoever he is — will be yours."

"If he survives," Rox gulped.

"A pinch of rat's skull always helps."

"Rat skull," Rox repeated, suddenly cold. "Do they do that at the supermarket?"

Mrs Baldock ignored her.

They had reached Maze Hill gate where an ice-cream van was parked as usual. As soon as he saw it, Georgie started begging for a lolly.

"No!" Rox growled, walking on. She was getting worried but they were so close to home, they'd be safe inside their own front door in five minutes.

Georgie picked up a lolly stick from the ground and started poking Rox with it to get her attention. "I want a lolly!" he whinged.

Rox was trying to catch his hand to make a run for it but he kept dancing away. "Georgie," Rox shouted.

"No you don't!" Mrs Baldock announced. She grabbed Georgie's hand and pushed them both down the hill to their left.

Chapter Fifteen

They were standing together in front of an arched door in the abbey wall. It was draped in ivy.

"This isn't right," Rox muttered.

Mrs Baldock gave the door a hefty kick.

"Where are we going now?" Georgie asked, trying to pull his hand free.

"Where's this?" Rox asked, as the door crashed open. She was looking at a silent, dripping, brambly place they'd never seen before.

Rox cleared her throat. They had to get away from Mrs Baldock. "I think we'll just go straight home now," she said.

The old woman switched on a strange, sweet voice.

"But this *is* home. Anyway don't you want to see something fascinating first?" she asked and tugged Georgie through the doorway.

Rox had no choice. She had to follow.

Georgie grew more and more bewildered. He was stumbling along the path, trying hard to memorise every stick and stone. Left and right, right and left they went. Soon they were drenched and completely lost. He had a maddening feeling that home wasn't far away but where? He hadn't liked Mrs Baldock before today and he liked her a lot less now. She seemed so different, not at all like the person who was Gran's friend and who'd given Rox a book. It was all such a jumble in his head that he was sure of only one thing — this was all Rox's fault.

"My feet are all wet," Rox said, "and these brambles are nasty. We shouldn't have followed her."

"It was your stupid idea," Georgie pointed out. "I want to go home."

They finally stopped at a grizzled stone building. Mrs Baldock pushed them through a door and up a dark stairway.

"Have you never seen the back of the abbey before?" Mrs Baldock hissed.

"This is the abbey?" Rox asked.

The old woman opened the door into a murky room and forced Rox inside.

Rox protested, "Leave off!" but found herself staring at the old woman's long, thin finger. It was pointing to the single, arched window.

"Go on!" the old woman rasped. "Look!"

Rox walked to the window as if it was actually her idea and rubbed a patch clean. She couldn't believe what she saw.

"We're here!" she spluttered. "We're home!"

The old woman laughed, that same crackling laugh that fried up their chests so they couldn't breathe properly.

Georgie was still hovering near the door. He was watching the old woman's hands, wringing and wind- ing over each other like worms. Her whisper beside him made him jump.

"Nobody's here except us Georgie," she hissed. "It's our secret. Until you admit it."

"Admit what?" Georgie whispered. She couldn't mean his picture. Tim had got it back from her flat before she'd seen it. Then Gran had heard about it and *she'd* gone down and shown it to Mrs Baldock and they'd had a good laugh about it. Mrs Baldock had really seemed not to mind.

He felt the old woman push him and he stumbled inside. Rox whipped around just as the door clicked shut. A key turned and they heard the old witch stamping down the stairs.

*   *   *

The smell was the worst. It was a sweet, decaying smell that Georgie had come across only once before. It had been in hospital when he'd visited Grandpa for the last time. In the hospital the smell had been hidden a bit by cleaning stuff and flowers but here nothing got in its way.

"I don't like this, Georgie," Rox said, "That's not our Mrs Baldock. No way."

"I don't think it is either. And what does she mean, admit it?" he said, "I haven't done anything!"

"I know you haven't."

They hugged each other. Then Rox kissed the top of his head, "Come on, time for action. Nobody's going to kidnap us!"

They shouted and thumped on the door, the window, the walls and the floor.

Nothing happened.

Then Georgie felt a drip run down his ankle. He pulled up his trouser and found a bramble scratch, oozing blood down his shin.

"Rox?" he moaned.

Rox sat down on the floor beside him.

"It's filthy," she said. "What can we clean it with? I know!" She ripped a page from *The Winsome Two-some*, folded and spat on it and started dabbing Georgie's shin.

"I hope the real Mrs Baldock doesn't mind," Rox said. "The paper's lovely and soft though. It says 'The End'."

"Is this the end of us?" Georgie asked. His voice was very small.

"Don't be ridiculous. They'll find us soon. Listen to this: 'What a jolly jape,' Dorothy ejaculated.'"

"What does that mean?"

"I haven't a clue." Rox said, hugging Georgie. "There's more, listen: 'Oh Neville,' she squeaked, 'I thought we'd never be free. How clever of you to knock the key out onto the paper with your penknife and pull it back under the door.' Hey, that's brilliant!"

Rox squinted through the keyhole.

"Where's that lolly stick you were poking me with? Give it here!"

Distant stamping in the stairwell suggested that Mrs Baldock was on her way back.

"Hurry up Georgie," Rox hissed as he handed it over. "Perfect. We're getting out of here."

The footsteps were getting close. Rox tore two joined pages carefully from the book, flattened them and pushed them under the door.

"When we get free," she said, "we'll run so hard past Mrs Baldock that she won't be able to hold us. If she grabs one of us, the other one has to pull with every ounce of his or her strength until we both get away."

"Okay," Georgie said, standing up.

Rox wiggled his lolly stick through the keyhole. With a ting, the key fell and Rox drew the pages and the key back into the room.

There was no other word for it. It was amazing. As the steps got closer they unlocked the door and ran out into – their own bright landing at home.

They stood there panting and holding hands, not knowing what to say. On the wall were pictures of them all on holiday last year. There was the open door to Rox's room, showing its usual mess and on the other side was the door of the chapel and the little toilet. There were Dad's books on shelves up to the ceiling. Georgie had opened one once and seen a picture of a woman with nothing on, and got told off for it. Oddest of all, behind them, where they had just stepped through the doorway, was a smooth, stone wall.

The Winsome Twosome fell open in Rox's hand and she read out: "'Oh Neville,' she squeaked, 'I thought we'd never be free.'" The page was securely sewn into the book. In fact all the pages were sewn in – in the right order.

Georgie didn't care. He was home and he was safe. He ran down the landing screaming, "Mum!"

Chapter Sixteen

As soon as Mum heard about the kidnap she stormed round to Mrs Baldock and pitched straight in. What was Mrs Baldock doing frightening the wits out of her children, what wits they had anyway?

Georgie was hiding with Dad but Rox hurried after her, keen to see if there was going to be a fight.

Mrs Baldock looked shocked.

"How could I frighten anyone?" she asked.

"Okay, put it another way," Mum said. "What have you been doing today?"

"Well," Mrs Baldock replied, "in the morning one of my Henrys gave birth to 19 babies. Want to come in and see?"

Rox shivered. Mice. This was more like the Mrs Baldock they all knew, and that Gran for one was growing to love. Not a bit like the Mrs Baldock at the fair. Or was it? Could she have been acting? If she had been, was she acting then or now? Maybe a test would be a good idea?

"Then after lunch I read your grandmother's Tarot Cards," Mrs Baldock went on. "It was quite a session, three hours. She's a good laugh, is Dora."

"Didn't you say she's a stupid old twit?" Rox asked.
Mum glared.

"Not me," Mrs Baldock said. "I'd never say that. I think she's being very brave."

"So you haven't been to the fair at Blackheath?" Mum asked.

"Nah. I hate fairs. Why'd you ask?"

"I hate them too," Mum said. "Rox and Georgie must have made a mistake but I think we need your help."

"Come on in and tell me all about it," Mrs Baldock invited and led the way into her kitchen.

Rox followed. She watched as Mrs Baldock filled her tin kettle and settled it on her hob beside a mouse cage. Very gently the old woman parted the clouds of chewed newspaper inside to show Rox nineteen newborn mice huddled together like mini-sausages. Rox was surprised to feel a surge of tenderness.

"Once years ago I lifted one out on its first day," Mrs Baldock said, "just to welcome it, and do you know what?"

"What?" Rox asked, surprisingly interested.

"The mother ate it."

Mrs Baldock tucked the babies' cover back safely. "So we'll not bother them too much today."

"She's lovely," Mum whispered to Rox, "it couldn't have been her." Mum turned to Mrs Baldock, "So you're a white witch?"

Mrs Baldock nodded.

"Would you run to a spell to make money?" Mum asked, "so we could put something by for a rainy day."

"What you put by for a rainy day is your wellies. I do white magic, dear. Not miracles."

But Rox was still not 100 percent sure. Not after what she had been through. Just one more test.

"I bet you do a love spell though," she said. "To make a person fall in love with a person." Mum was staring at Rox.

"A love spell is a doddle," Mrs Baldock said. "Stick two pins through a red candle at dawn, on a Tuesday, when the moon is in Venus, and when the candle burns down to the pins, your destined love will come to you."

"Is that it?"

"Yep."

"No womb of hare? No rat skulls?"

"You can surround your candle with the bones of a mature vixen if you like," the white witch laughed, "but rat skulls have been hard to come by since we joined the European Union."

"Mum," Rox interrupted Mum's hoots of laughter. "Mum! Shut up and listen. I asked the Mrs Baldock in the park about a love spell and she went on about rat's skull and womb of hare. The more I listen to you, Mrs Baldock, the more I'm sure I was right and it wasn't you at the fair at all!"

"Of course it wasn't, dear."

"Who was it then? Or what?" Rox's voice was unusually high. She was starting to get scared again.

"An apparition," the old woman said. "It appeared to be me. Ghosts do that sometimes. Cheek! What you need's a spell. A real belter. I'll come over just before midnight and do one."

A memory flickered in Rox's mind of a photograph on the day of the eclipse, of a certain person exposing more than her good nature. She had to ask, "I was wondering . . . eh . . . I just want to know, will you be wearing any . . . are you . . . eh . . . clothes?"

Mum glared at Rox but Mrs Baldock just raised one bushy grey eyebrow.

"You mean am I going to be skyclad?" she said, "You'll have to wait and see."

*   *   *

Georgie had never been up so late. The minute Mrs Baldock came into the house, he'd run to hide under the kitchen table. Rox joined him under there and explained that this Mrs Baldock was not the person who'd kidnapped them and that everything was going to be alright now. By the time Mrs Baldock and Rox had taken him to see the baby mice, he was convinced.

But Dad was not. He kept stamping about saying, "Have we all gone stark staring mad?"

Mum ignored him and turned off all the lights. She unplugged the television and video recorder and the phone. By five minutes to midnight the whole family including Gran sat in the candlelight, waiting.

Mrs Baldock arrived, in a purple tracksuit, lugging a big, brown suitcase.

"Coming for your holidays, Mrs B?" Dad asked.

"A sceptic in our midst! Mr Exworth, I wonder could you please fetch me a bowl of salt and a glass of white wine?" she asked.

Dad pulled himself up to his full height, as if he was not used to being bossed about in his own home. "I think I can lay my hands on a cheeky little Chardonnay for you. Anything else? French fries? How about a karate chop?"

At the mention of karate chop Tim started. It was as if Big Danny had just breathed on his neck.

Mum led Dad into the kitchen, explaining that Mrs Baldock was only here to help. Rox confirmed that the entire house was unplugged, undisturbed and peaceful.

"No negative forces must disturb our ritual," Mrs Baldock declared and opened the suitcase.

Rox glanced at Tim and smirked. Mrs Baldock put a white robe on over her tracksuit and produced several boxes of candles. Rox was instructed to light one candle in every window of the house.

"I make them myself," she said. "I consecrate them with a light dressing of oil during the waxing of the moon. The candle is an image of humanity."

Tim made a mental note for the WYSIWYG file. His first reaction had been to stay well clear of this non-sense. The only magic he could see was watching every-body's common sense disappear. Then he remembered the lard and shivered. Something useful just might crop up.

"The wax is the physical body," Mrs Baldock went on, "the wick is the mind and the flame is our spirit or soul. Light them in every room now, Rox, especially the chapel, and that little toilet of yours beside it. I have a feeling. I don't know . . ."

Rox headed off with Georgie carrying half the candles for her.

Mrs Baldock raised both her palms above her shoulders and murmured, "The Goddess is alive! Magick is afoot! Blessed be!"

"And God bless me!" Gran echoed.

Tim wanted to do the lighting bit but his job was to set up the altar. It was a folding table covered by an embroidered cloth on which Mrs Baldock laid a huge, silver sword with a curly hilt.

"Go and ask your father where he's got to with that salt," she ordered.

By the time Tim came back with the wine and salt she was burning something in a brass bowl that filled the room with peppery scent.

"Where's the wine?" Mrs Baldock barked. "Sorry I'm getting irritable but I can feel our friend's presence. He doesn't like me being here. Now we need to know exactly when it's midnight."

"According to my watch it's already four minutes past," Tim grinned, as he headed off to call everyone back.

"Oh Goddess!" Mrs Baldock blazed. "I better get cracking."

As Rox, Mum and Georgie all rushed to the altar she threw back her head and shouted, "PROTECTED MAY THIS HOUSEHOLD BE. DONG!"

"What's she trying to do," Dad muttered to Tim, as he crept back into the room, "turn herself into a church clock?"

Tim snorted with laughter.

"CLEANSED OF NEGA-TIVI-TEE, DONG! I'm being the bells of midnight," she explained. "DONG!"

She seized her sword in both hands and chanted, "BLESSED BE – DONG! – SO MOTE IT BE! – DONG!"

Dad flinched as she swung around clockwise and blessed him.

"That's enough in here, dears. Bring the altar, Tim! Come along Rox." She stomped off to repeat the lot in the kitchen, the dining room and every room in the house.

"If she as much as breathes in my den, she's dead meat," Dad growled to Mum, as they passed through the hall again.

"Where's the den, Tim?" Mrs Baldock whispered.

"Already done it."

"Good."

*   *   *

"Whew! I hope we haven't used up all that wine," Mrs Baldock said, as she subsided into a chair in the kitchen half an hour later and put her feet up. "What about the workers?"

Gran poured her friend a glass. "Here, Fuschia, you deserve it."

But Mrs Baldock was on her feet again. "I nearly forgot," she said. "I haven't done the outside! Come on, everybody. This is the best bit."

They all trooped out to the front garden. Georgie was draped over Dad's shoulder, half-asleep.

"I'm only coming out for the exercise," Dad protested but was as fascinated as anybody.

Tim steadied the table under the oak tree in the front garden. The night was cloudy and dreadfully dark. Candles sparkling in every window gave the house a weird look, and the children shivered in their dressing gowns. Mrs Baldock gathered up her sword

108

for the last time, swung it over her head three times and bellowed at the top of her voice, "BLESSED BE THIS HOUSE! – DONG! – AND ALL WHO ENTER HEREIN – DONG!"

Beyond the topmost branches of the oak tree the moon floated free and draped them all in silver light. Every room of the house shone in the light of a tiny orange flame – except one. Beyond the little lavatory, next to the chapel, a single arched window on the first floor was still dark.

Tim whistled through his teeth, "WYSIWYG – the missing window!"

As they stared at the window every person on the lawn distinctly saw something. It was a hooded head.

Chapter Seventeen

The next day Tim had rushed to his WYSIWYG file as soon as he woke and recorded every detail of what had happened. But he'd not dared go back to the file since. That was over a week ago. It was as if the file might haunt him or curse him or something.

Which was stupid, so he sat down at the laptop and stretched his fingers. He was going to look at the WYSIWYG file, sanely, sensibly, scientifically. Rox had to be kept well away. If she saw what he was doing, she would tease him forever.

He had learned a new word that day and typed it in and what it meant. *Dichotomy: the phase of the moon where exactly half of the disc appears to shine, reflecting the sun's light. Also, any decision where the choice between two opposites is difficult or impossible.*

What Tim had seen last Saturday night was a dichotomy alright. He couldn't get it out of his head. Mrs Baldock's white magic was obviously daft but they'd all been drawn in by it at the time, even Dad. The fact was that they were all decidedly spooked. Rox reckoned that somebody had died a horrible death in the abbey and somehow the walls recorded it and kept playing it back. She might be right. But as a scientist he had to examine the evidence sensibly. The only tangible fact he had so far was that WYSIWYG 2 was embarrassingly long. Time to sort the rubbish from the serious evidence. He scrolled down the items:

DATE	NAME	PLACE	PHENOMENON
25 Aug	*Rox and Tim*	*staircase*	*voice says "Admit it!" and she hears a thump*

Explanation: Rox. Lively imagination. Lives and breathes daft ghost stories.
DELETE.

| *30 Aug– 6 Sept* | *Tim* | *bed* | *'lard, lard' visitor.* |

Explanation: Be honest now. Face it. Dreams.
DELETE.

| *6 Sept* | *Tim* | *laptop* | *WYSIWYG file gone.* |

Explanation: No trouble there either: Rox fiddling with the laptop.
DELETE.

| *6 Sept* | *Rox* | *sleepover* | *nearly pulled off balcony (not hard enough)* |

Explanation: Girly hysteria, as above.
DELETE.

| *7 Sept* | *Gran* | *her flat* | *Mrs B's rhyme finds her cereal.* |

Explanation: Coincidence.
DELETE.

DATE	NAME	PLACE	PHENOMENON
8 Sept	Gran	Mrs B's flat	Séance with Grandpa.

Tim sighed as he looked at this last one. The fact was that ever since the séance, Gran had been a lot happier. This deserved a more sensitive approach.

Explanation: Wishful thinking on Gran's part? Kindness on Mrs Baldock's? And who could blame them.
DELETE.

| 8 Sept | Mum | chapel | hears scratching. |

Explanation: See Rox's thump in the hall.
DELETE.

| 13 Sept | Rox & Georgie | fair | R & G 'kidnapped' & magically returned. |

Explanation: Pure attention seeking.
DELETE.

| 13 Sept | Mrs B | whole flat | exorcism/hooded head. |

Explanation: A shadow. Nothing else made sense.
DELETE.

That was over a week ago and since then, nothing.

So that took care of that. One empty WYSIWYG 2 file. What you see is what you get and there was no earthly reason for any of them to be afraid.

Mind you that hadn't stopped the whole family sleeping in the same bedroom every night since Mrs Baldock's exorcism. Rox was the worst. She kept dreaming she was locked in a coffin and couldn't sleep until she'd moved Dad out of the double bed and was tucked in beside Mum.

It was the same that night.

Typical, Tim thought, and curled deeper inside his sleeping bag on the floor. *She takes all the privileges.* Somebody fell over his feet.

"What are you doing up?" he asked.

"Homework," Rox whispered.

"At half-past five in the morning?"

Rox smoothed her hair away from her eyes, "I've got a test tomorrow. I didn't want to disturb you."

"Do you ever," Dad said, moving his arm from under Georgie's head. "Why aren't you in your own beds, you lot?"

"Tony!" Mum was awake now too, "you *know* why!"

"Because we're terrified witless that some spectre's going to come in the night and steal them? Nobody would steal these children. Look at them!"

"Be serious," Mum said.

"I *am*. Aren't we a ghost-free zone now?" Dad sneered. "Or was all that Baldock business nothing but mumbo jumbo? *Jumbo* mumbo jumbo?"

"She meant well," Mum said.

"*Meant* well? Meant *well*?" Even in the dark Tim could see that Dad was turning dangerously purple. "She comes in here. Bosses us about. Drinks our wine and then, after she's supposed to have done her stuff, *after* mind you, she persuades us we've seen a ghost in a room that doesn't even exist!"

"It does exist."

"Where?" Dad splayed his hands. "Take me to it. Now. Why not?"

"The ghost put me and Rox in there," Georgie said and crept in beside Mum for a cuddle.

"She's bad for the children too," Dad shouted. "The more she's here, the more spooky rubbish they make up."

"We're not making it up!" Rox whined.

"Okay Tony, prove it. Get a proper exorcist," Mum said, sitting-up, "one with qualifications. They must exist. Look in the yellow pages."

"We don't need an exorcist," Dad said. "We just need to behave like rational human beings."

"Then let's talk about it in the daylight," Mum sighed. "Get back to bed, Rox. There's no test that needs this much fuss."

"But," Rox was twisting the sleeve of her dressing gown, "there's this other thing too. Gran and I started it off last night but . . . Ti-im," she wheedled, "I need the bones of a mature vixen. Where have you put Tyrannosaurus Fox?"

"Oh no!" Mum clapped both hands over her ears. "Don't tell me the moon's in Venus!"

"And it's Tuesday before dawn. We're setting up my love spell and we need those bones."

Tim told her were to find them. It was no skin off his nose if she wanted to make a fool of herself, in every possible way.

While Rox vanished with the wherewithal for her love spell, Tim followed Dad and Georgie down the cold stairs. Dad had whispered that they could sneak in a few fried eggs before Mum got up. Tim was about to say that they tasted even better in the dark, when the front door rattled.

"What was that?" Dad whispered.

Rox rushed down the stairs so fast she yelped as hot wax spilt on her hand. Her candle trailed a coil of smoke behind her.

"Somebody's at the front door," she grinned, as she tidied her eyebrows with a damp finger. "And I think I know who it might be . . ."

"I'll go!" Dad announced. "At six in the morning it's nobody sane."

Rox pushed Dad out of the way. It had to be Jack. She rushed along the hall, her face shimmering in the light cast by the 'love' candle.

Dad raced along behind and beat her to the front door by a few centimetres He threw it open wide.

"And *what* do you think *you're* doing?" he shouted.

Mr MacFadyen stood in the half-light with a screwdriver in one hand. His other was cupped around the base of their outdoor lamp. His face twisted in embarrassment as he muttered, "Oh! Just . . . you know"

"No! I don't!" Dad roared.

"It's this lamp! It's a horror, Mr Exworth, admit it."

"That doesn't mean you can help yourself to it!"

"But next to a fine old door like that, Mr Exworth!"

Dad was about to say something unwise about the door and Mr MacFadyen's head, when Rox's candle crackled in the hall and went out.

"Oh no!" Rox gasped, one hand at her throat.

"What's wrong?" Dad barked.

"AAAARRRGH!" Rox was rolling her eyes.

"WHAT?" they all shouted.

Rox recovered enough to speak, "It means that Mr MacFadyen is my destined love!"

Chapter Eighteen

An hour later Dad was using his firm but fair voice on the telephone, "This *is* an emergency. Thank you."

He returned to his second breakfast — skimmed yoghurt.

"The church exorcist is coming this afternoon. He doesn't work after dark so I'll come home early. I happen to think that a decent night's sleep is all we need," he said, forcing down the yoghurt, "but that seems to be too much to ask."

Mum breezed in.

"You won't forget to tell him about the fried eggs," she said.

Dad's eyes swivelled. "What fried eggs?" he muttered.

"Can't you smell it?" Mum sucked her teeth, not fooled. "Somebody's been frying eggs. Must be the ghost. Tim, you put that in your spook file: ghost likes fried eggs. Because nobody else . . ." she hissed, glaring straight at Dad, ". . . is allowed to have them."

Dad looked sheepish, then went on the attack. He stalked into the hall and swept Rox's candles and sticks on the floor.

"What's this rubbish doing here on my shelf?" he growled.

"Dad!" Rox shouted. "That's my spell."

"Not here it's not."

"Gran put it there. To get the dawn light."

"Then it can take up space in Gran's flat," he said. "Anyway hasn't it worked already? Isn't Mr MacFadyen THE ONE?"

Rox ignored him. It was the only way sometimes.

Dad marched to the door, stopped and stamped back into the kitchen. "Roxanne," he said, "Why are you doing homework?"

Rox grunted, "I told you, history test. I hate history, where's the future in it?"

"In that case," Dad was getting excited, "put that book away. I've got an idea and I need your help."

Tim and Mum glanced at each other. Was it time to take cover?

"Why me?" Rox squeaked.

"We've got to break into that secret room and only you, my girl, have the power to help. Get on the phone *now* to your destined love. We can't sort this out until we get into that room, and we can't do that without MacFadyen. Get him and his clipboard back here today."

Rox gave a huge sob, "He's *not* my destined love, Dad, you're horrible!"

She flew up the stairs, a pink tissue pressed to both eyes.

Dad shrugged, "What?"

"Tony," Mum said as she followed Rox upstairs, "sometimes you go too far."

* * *

Tim leant against a wall in a sunny corner of the playground. If he'd dared to bring his skateboard he'd have been working on his ollie, the way he did every minute he could at home, but today he was deep in a book. Its front cover was missing and the pages were all curled. When Gran had said, "This was your Grandpa's favourite book of poems," Tim had thought, *Boring*.

At first glance it was exactly as he expected, a lot of complicated words piled all over each other. But as his thumbs stroked the soft pages Grandpa had once held, the book kept falling open at the same page. He felt something in the margin and realised it was the imprint of a thumbnail — Grandpa's thumbnail — next to one of the most peculiar poems of all, *Byzantium* by WB Yeats:

Before me floats an image, man or shade,
Shade more than man, more image than a shade;

Goosepimples erupted down Tim's back. Too spooky. He closed the book fast. A skateboard rattled over and almost cracked his ankle.

"Timmy Four-eyes! Better at reading than skating?" Big Danny poked Tim's ribs.

Danny raised a knee in the direction of Tim's fly without making contact. Tim couldn't help flinching all the same.

Pitbull Pete sniggered.

"What you got there?" Danny grabbed the book and held it high. "Ha ha! Look what Timmy Four-eyes has got! Poems!"

The whole playground laughed. Tim tingled with fear as the book fell open in Danny's hand and the laughing died away. Danny studied the pages in silence.

Somebody dared to shout, "Hey look, Danny's reading poems!"

Danny shouted straight back, "I am *not*!"

Tim murmured, "I can see that — you're not moving your lips."

Danny shot him a glare.

"What you say?" he snarled.

"I said," Tim said, meeting Danny's eye. "Give it back."

Somebody sniggered. Danny whipped round to see a girl covering her mouth. He shoved the book back at Tim.

"Read it," Danny ordered, folding his beefy arms. "I like a laugh."

Like a man about to step into a piranha tank, Tim breathed in and leafed through the book. All he needed was something to save his life. *Consider the grass growing*, he read. Not today thank you. Or this? — *We borrowed the loan of Kerr's big ass*. Tim could imagine what they'd make of that. Come on, Grandpa, Tim pleaded silently, I need your help here.

The book flopped open again, at the page with the thumbnail mark:

A mouth that has no moisture and no breath,
Breathless mouths may summon;
I hail the superman;
I call it death-in-life and life-in-death.

120

Tim hadn't a clue what it meant but there was something beautiful in those words that summed everything up. He straightened his glasses and read aloud.

There was an embarrassed silence when he finished. Then Danny poked Tim in the chest, "You think you're Superman?"

Tim's hand moved to Danny's chest before he could think.

"Maybe," he said and shoved Danny. He amazed himself, he actually *pushed* Danny. It was a truly fine moment. Until Danny pushed him back.

"You think you're hard?" Danny said, "We'll see if you're hard. See me here tomorrow. 13.05 hours. Right?"

"13.05 hours," Tim repeated. His confidence ebbed as he breathed out. He had actually agreed to fight Big Danny. He could end up in hospital. He rolled Grandpa's spanner nervously in his pocket and was suddenly inspired.

"For a contest?" he asked.

"A whah?" Big Danny demanded.

"A contest. Skateboard," Tim's voice faltered, "if you think you're up to it . . ."

Big Danny grinned. "A skateboard contest? Me?" He stuck out his arms and wobbled on one leg. "And *you*?"

Danny rolled away laughing. Which seemed to mean yes. Which seemed to mean that though Tim's guts were churning at least he'd had the choice of weapons.

* * *

Having a choice is more than he got when he and Rox were deciding who should be closest to the keyhole. It was late that afternoon and the exorcist had arrived. He and Dad were talking in the sitting room.

"I'm the one doing the WYSIWYG database," Tim said.

"I was here first," she replied.

Tim couldn't fight logic like that.

"What does he look like then?" he asked.

"Big."

"Big-tall or big-fat?"

"Both. A real two-chair priest. Yep, there's Dad bringing him the second chair. Now he's . . . he's opening his briefcase."

"What's in it?" Tim could hardly wait to hear.

"The usual probably. Bibles. Holy water. Garlic." Her sudden intake of breath raised the hairs on Tim's neck. "It's this blue tube, plastic, about three inches long. He's putting it to his lips."

"Some ancient instrument for driving out demons?"

"No," she giggled, "it's his asthma inhaler."

"Open the door a bit so we can hear."

Tim had to crouch so that Rox could see over his head.

"And after you were bullied at school, Mr Exworth, did your relationship with your Dad alter at all?"

Dad stared out the window.

"Forgive me if I seem rude, Father," he said, "but I'd love to know how my Dad has anything to do with this. I thought you were an exorcist. Have I got it wrong?"

"No, not at all. It's just, well usually once we've got the old worries off your chest, Bob's your uncle. No need for the *Our Father* backwards or stakes through anybody's heart. That's the way we work these days."

"You mean there's nothing haunted about this place?" Dad asked happily.

The priest scratched his stubbly chin. "It's a fine place. You can feel the holiness. Must have cost a fortune in damp-proofing alone," he grinned.

Scratch, scratch.

Fear prickled down Tim's spine. Was this what Mum had heard in the chapel, that time? Or was it Rox?

The priest's hands splayed on his chubby knees but the scratching continued.

"I'm not saying it's not haunted, Mr Exworth," he went on regardless. "It's just that, well, it usually isn't. Thirty years I've been at this job and not once have I seen anything that couldn't be sorted out with a bit of a chinwag."

"Didn't you hear that scratching?" Dad insisted. "Just now and when we were up in the chapel. Like fingernails or something."

"Now, Mr Exworth, are our imaginations running away with us?"

"Well, what did it sound like to you?"

The priest produced a large handkerchief and blew his nose.

"May I suggest," he said, "with the benefit of thirty years experience in these matters, that you have . . . rats in your loft."

Tim punched the air and went, "Yesss!"

123

Of course! It was as simple as that. WYSIWYG! There were no ghosts.

Rox was muttering that the priest was an idiot. But as soon as he was gone, Dad and Tim swapped high fives.

Chapter Nineteen

After dinner, Rox lay back in a hot bath. There couldn't really be rats running about in the loft only a few metres above her. Could there? She breathed in trying to relax — four drops of marjoram oil for relaxation and two of sage. She had decided against rosemary oil for remembrance. What she wanted was to forget.

They all laughed now when she told them about her dreams, or nightmares more like. Tim laughed the loudest of the lot, so she'd told everyone they had stopped. So they had, the coffin ones. But there was another dream. It was more about anger than fear, and all the more worrying for it. Last night's was so weird it had been bothering her all day. Perhaps a bath would wash it away or at least clear her thoughts.

Tim was in it. Sort of. It was as if she knew it was him and yet it wasn't him. She'd been needling him all day, as you do, and there she was doing it again in the dream except that this time it was no fun. She was spying on his homework, looking at a yellow page lying on his desk. He had been writing Latin words inside a frame of green and blue painted leaves, blending into curls of orange flame. She had stood staring at the desk, feeling cold and exhausted, and for some reason she was bursting with rage. Suddenly all these words started coming out of her mouth in a deep voice that wasn't hers:

"So here it is. Your precious work. With all your reeds and beads and inks and stinks. And what do you paint? **Pater Noster**, Our Father. Look at that P, it is made of two fish! There is **Sed libera nos a malo**, deliver us from evil, and your S is a fish! Even in **Etne nos inducas in tentationem**, lead us not into temptation, your E frames Jonah, up to his arms in fish! Where is the bread, Brother Scribe? The bread, the staff of life? You render our Lord's prayer for daily bread with such beauty but you fill it up with fish!"

Rox looked at the reflection of her toes in the water at the end of the bath. She hadn't a clue why she should dream about bread and fish but it had felt so real. The deep voice kept churning in her brain . . .

You need a reminder of what Our Lord said on the subject. 'Take, eat,' said Our Lord, 'this is my body'. My artistry cannot equal yours but look at what I do, **in libera** I will dot your letter 'i' with a little loaf. Delicious. And in **inducas in tentationem**, I will draw you a tasty, little bread roll above each 'i'. I only want to help you. You must eat your bread, Brother Scribe. You must not fast and slowly die. Because the baking of bread is holy work too, you know. My holy work. Are you too proud to hold my bread in your inky fingers? Pride, Brother Scribe, is the first of the deadly sins, is it not? Admit your pride, Brother Scribe, ADMIT IT!"

Rox sat up in the bath and stared at the chapel's vaulted ceiling. Weird! If only she could get it out of her mind. *Admit it!* She'd heard it before. Said like that. When she and Georgie were being kidnapped in the mystery room, the fake Mrs Baldock had said, *Admit it!* in exactly that voice.

Rox shivered and sent ripples criss-crossing the bath water. Time to be under a nice big duvet, she thought – Mum and Dad's duvet.

* * *

Even before the storm started, Tim was having a job sleeping. He was back in his own bed but he kept dreaming that he was locked in one of the school lockers with a football. It kept growing and growing until Tim was being pressed against the walls of the locker and soon there would be no room for him at all. Every time he shouted for help, the football shouted too and its voice – its voice was Big Danny's.

Lightning glimmered through his window. He got up, wrapped the curtains round his head and stared outside. The next flash was coming. He knew because his hair was standing on end. Yes, the garden lit up.

His hair stood even higher. There were footsteps behind him.

"My electric's gone, so I thought I'd come and see you, love. The other two are in bed with your mum and dad."

It was Gran.

"Do you know what your Grandpa always did in a storm?" she asked. "He held his nose."

"Why?"

"He said it helped."

Another colossal crash thudded against the abbey.

"Dere. Dat's better, is'd id?" Gran winked.

"I like to watch, Gran."

Tim pulled back the curtains and waited for the next flash. He heard a tummy rumble.

"Excuse me," he said.

"I dought id was me."

Gran came closer and hugged Tim from behind. That feeling was with him again. They were not alone. But it was not a frightening sensation. In fact Tim could almost smell Grandpa, he felt so close.

Gran sighed, "I feel very encouraged by Mrs Baldock's powers, you know? I can't say so to your mother but it's as if your Grandpa is with me all the time. Do you know what I mean, darling?"

"Yes," Tim said. "I do."

Gran kissed the top of his head and they stood there together, the two of them – or was it three? – until the storm passed and they went back to bed.

*   *   *

Tim could have done with some company, dead or alive, as he walked into the boys' toilets next morning at break-time.

Big Danny was there, of course, and immediately kicked his skateboard up into his hand. From the corner of Tim's eye it looked bigger and meaner than ever, like a shark edged with razor wire. Big Danny ignored the urinal and peed in the washbasin.

"Like I was saying," he said, tapping his forehead, "skateboarding is in here. State of mind. Not some

128

wannabe in a baseball cap, worn sideways, reading poems."

Tim took off his hat and stuffed it up his jumper. Grandpa's book was safe at home.

A voice came from one of the cubicles – Pitbull Pete.

"Your hardflip, Dan, isn't that just a frontside kick-flip shove-it?" he asked.

Danny zipped himself and turned to face Tim. Danny was at least a head taller than Tim, which gave Tim an excellent view of his nostrils.

"Let's ask Timmy here, what's a hardflip?"

Tim's mouth opened but nothing came out.

"I seen you in the park," Danny said. "Your board's supposed to stick to your feet, you know, for an ollie, not slop all over the show. It's not an ollie if it don't stick to your feet."

Danny emphasised his point by crashing the edge of his board down onto Tim's toes, "Come *on*, Timmy, what's a hardflip?"

Pitbull Pete swung out of his cubicle and stood behind him. Tim needed to stay cool. He *was* cool. So cool he was shivering.

He stared up at Big Danny. If he was going to get blamed for fighting, he might as well do it instead of being squashed like a fly.

"Isn't it like a bothside nosepick?" he asked and jammed two fingers up his own nostrils to show what he meant. For an extra flourish he stuck out his tongue. He regretted it the minute Big Danny slapped his chin upward.

"You ready then?" Danny asked.

"Yeah," Tim said keeping his voice steady, tasting blood.

"Danny Superman against Timmy the Wimp?" Pitbull Pete was dancing about, punching the air, "*Mashing* Timmy the Wimp? *Slaughtering* him?"

Tim turned to the door. It was time to think with his legs. But at a nod from Big Danny, Pitbull Pete grabbed Tim's arms. Danny stepped forward and used his own huge shoes to painfully anchor Tim's feet to the floor. Tim stiffened his back and lifted his chin. He couldn't kick. He couldn't punch. But he could, if necessary, spit.

"Come on, guys," Tim grunted. "Don't you ever get bored with this?"

"Who said I was going to hurt you?"

Big Danny held the bridge of Tim's glasses in place for two seconds, then removed them and put them in his own trouser pocket: "Just evening up the odds a bit."

As if Danny's odds could be any better — he was at least a head taller than Tim and twice as broad.

Pitbull Pete tightened his grip on Tim's arms.

Danny's wide fuzzy mouth opened again, "Don't forget. 13.05 hours. Tomorrow."

"Hang on, it's today."

"Nah. Can't be bothered today. You'll have to wait."

At a nod from Danny, Pitbull Pete released Tim's arms. They both shoved him casually into the wall as they left the toilets. Tim felt ridiculously happy to see them go. He was free and he was still breathing. But by the time he'd rubbed feeling back into his arms he realised that things were worse than ever. On top of everything else he'd lost his glasses and he had no spares. He'd have to ask Mum to buy new ones the minute he got home. And if Mum was too busy for him to get a word in, Rox would have to ask for him. Probably making sure she did it with the biggest fuss possible.

Chapter Twenty

Rox slung her school bag down the hall, sat on the stairs and opened her magazine at the problem page. It was just what she needed after that disastrous history test. After so many nightmares she could hardly see the test, let alone think of the answers.

She skimmed through the headlines: *Fabbo Dream-boy*. Ah. Here was something she did know about:

> *Dear Hannah Heartfixer,*
> *I'm so mizz! My fabbo dream-boy doesn't seem to know I exist. He like spends his whole time playing Killer III on the computer. He took off his T-shirt once when I was talking to him so I know he loves me, but if I ever get the courage to talk to him, he doesn't talk back, he just grunts.*
> *Please help,*
> *Emma.*

Rox drew stubble and a long, luscious ponytail on the cartoon boy at the foot of the page, as she read Hannah Heartfixer's reply.

> *Dear Emma,*
> *Just relax. Be yourself. Giggle a lot and talk drivel (like me!) and he'll love you more than the soppiest puppy in no time.*
> *Good luck,*
> *Hannah Heartfixer.*

"Be myself. That's all there is to it," Rox smiled, as she tripped into the kitchen and went flying over a pile of toys.

"Georgie! What's this mess doing here?"

Georgie jumped out of a cardboard box on the floor.

Rox picked up a teething ring. "We haven't had all this out for ages," she said, "Look, there's my mooftie. Georgie? Did I hear you got into trouble today with Miss Thane?"

"A bit."

"Well?"

"She asked if we had any questions and I said, 'Did she know she had a whole lot of black hairs up her nose?'."

"I bet she liked that," Rox said.

"Yeah," Georgie grinned. "She went all red and everybody laughed."

A chuckle came from behind the washing machine. Mooftie hit the floor and Rox put on an entirely different voice.

"Oh Jack, hi! Can I make you a cup of tea or anything?" she smiled.

"Great, ta. Four sugars."

Rox put the kettle on.

"Georgie," Rox's oozy voice continued, "why don't you take all this upstairs and have a nice peaceful time in your bedroom. By yourself. Let's put it all in the box like this . . . "

Rox picked up a pink elephant and Georgie grabbed it. Rox held on tight.

"Give it to me!" Georgie yelled.

"Suit yourself," Rox hissed. She dropped the elephant and stepped over Georgie to find the tea bags.

Jack wriggled his hips and turned to look at whatever he was working on from the side. Rox gazed at his oily jeans and worn trainers. He had string instead of laces and frayed holes at his knees where hairy skin showed through. There was an unfamiliar lightness in Rox's head as she poured boiling water into his mug and stirred in the sugars. What would Hannah Heartfixer say? What would she do?

"Here's your tea, Jack," she giggled. Was she giggling enough?

Jack pushed himself away from the washing machine and sat up as Rox handed him the mug. His fingers brushed hers.

"Ta, love," he said smiling. He crawled back to his work.

Ta, love, he'd said. Ta, *love*. He'd said the L-word. To her. Rox couldn't have been in greater ecstasy.

"Rox, come here. Quick!!" Tim called from the hall.

"WHAT!" she bellowed. *There were times,* she thought, as she stamped off to find him, *that I could kill Tim stone dead.*

Tim had been hiding behind the sofa again so he could hear Mum settling in the latest exorcist. The curtains were drawn and a dozen candle flames shimmered in the sitting room mirror. If only exorcists could do something useful like exterminating Big Danny. Tim watched the Psychic Expert flip his grey plaits over his shoulders and point both index fingers heavenward. Then the incanting started.

Tim had just made it to the hall before the giggles got him.

"Rox!" he called again. "Quick! This is the funniest one yet!"

Rox was too nosey to stay angry and soon they were both hiding behind the sofa.

"Tell me everything," Tim whispered. His eyes were not good in this gloom and he couldn't face the inevitable fuss about his glasses – yet.

"Well . . ." Rox started. She stopped as tinkling and occasional fog horn sounds began to seep from a grimy tape machine on the floor between the crossed sandals of the Psychic Expert.

"My husband's not here at the moment," Mum said.

"Sssssshh!" The man sprayed spit over his tape machine. The machine gave a *hooop*, like a ship on the Thames.

"Oh, man!" he moaned. "How can I work with this noise? Can't you do something about the rats?"

"What rats?"

"Your pet rats," he said. "They keep scratching."

"We haven't got rats."

The man beat his breast and chanted: "They – Have – No – Rats!"

"What's happening?" Tim nudged Rox. "What's he doing?"

"Look, this is really my husband's department," Mum was saying. "Could you possibly come back tomorrow?"

"Lady, please. Let's not make this gig any easier for them."

135

"For who?" squeaked Mum.

"Exactly," boomed the man. His whole body shivered as if he'd just come out of the swimming pool and somebody had stolen his towel. He placed his palms flat on the floor beside his knees and began to tremble so violently that Mum stepped forward to help.

He misunderstood and walloped her on the arm, shouting, "Back, foul Devil."

"OY!" Mum hollered. "Who do you think you're hitting?"

The man stroked his long beard without apology. "Isn't that what I'm here to find out? What you have here is a serious case."

"Of what?"

"Demonic infestation, lady."

"Ghosts!" Rox breathed.

"And the sooner I'm out of it the better," the Psychic Expert went on. He rose in one fluid movement and gathered up his tape machine.

"Is that it?" Mum shrieked. "Are you leaving?"

"Too right. This is one heavy scene. Look at my hands. I need to be back home among my healing crystals right now. Make sure those candles do *not* go out before I'm off the premises."

"What about *us*?"

"Don't ask me, lady, I'm outta here."

They all watched the candle flames as the front door slammed and the Psychic Expert's car engine began to wheeze. After a while, the car's rhythmic coughing was replaced by rhythmic swearing and kicking of tyres.

Tim and Rox gazed from the window as the car finally began to roll out through the Abbey gates with the Psychic Expert half-pushing, half-hanging on.

Tim came out from behind the sofa and started blowing out the candles.

"You can't do that!" Rox yelled, standing up.

"Some demon's going to stop me are they?" Tim asked, carrying on. "Look . . . no demon."

Rox looked furious. She pointed back at him, "Look . . . no glasses!"

Mum turned on them both, hands on hips,

"And what are you two doing here?"

Tim and Rox looked thoroughly guilty.

"I didn't hear any scratching, Mum," Rox said, trying to distract her. "Did you hear scratching, Tim?"

"Nope," he said.

"No, I didn't either," Mum said and pursed her lips. "Demonic infestation! What a load of rubbish. That man was a total waste of money. Talking of which, has that plumber finished yet?"

"But Mum," Rox said, "the psychic man must have heard something."

Tim mimicked him, "I *soooo* need my healing crystals."

Mum looked suddenly at Tim,

"Where *are* your glasses? You've lost them!"

Tim said, no, he knew exactly where they were.

"Then go and get them," Mum said and strode off to the kitchen to give Jack a hard time. Rox followed her — any excuse.

If only it were that simple, Tim thought. He could hear Rox in the kitchen still arguing with Mum that surely the psychic man couldn't just make it up. Mum wasn't listening.

Who cares anyway, Tim thought as he escaped to his room and threw himself on his bed. He hadn't had any strange dreams in ages. Anyway a demonic infestation was nothing compared to being on his skateboard tomorrow, alone and toe-to-toe with Big Danny.

Chapter Twenty-One

Tim was in the middle of the playground with a crowd round him. He had been practising his ollies so much his knees ached. Sticking his bottom out the way Mum had shown him had helped a lot. He'd told her last night that he'd try and get his glasses back today but could she get him new spares anyway. She seemed to hear but he couldn't be sure.

There was no point worrying about that now. Big Danny was making his way through the crowd. Tim had mastered the art of ollying over a pencil, and had cleared a brick lying in the park once. But facing Big Danny, with an unnerving amount of blurred space around them both, was not the same. At least he had Grandpa's spanner in his pocket.

Tim decided to risk a reasonable request.

"Any chance of my glasses back?" he asked.

Danny pulled Tim's glasses from his pocket, put them on and started feeling his way round the yard. Girls were giggling. Boys chanted "Dah-nee! Dah-nee!"

Big Danny pocketed the glasses and raised his fist for silence. He flipped his board vertical, the way he always did before he launched into a trick. This time, instead of the board flowing into his hand, it wavered and crashed across Danny's shins.

"Ah! Ah! Ah!" Danny hopped around rubbing his legs.

Tim stepped forward. He was aware of Grandpa with him again, surrounding him with love. He mounted his board, stuck his bottom out and glided past Danny. Big Danny was still rolling in pain on the tarmac as Tim rolled, faster still, the length of the playground.

A football was lying in their penalty area. Could he jump it? Tim tested the spring in his knees. He'd never jumped anything so high. Somehow he felt good. His balance was right and Grandpa's voice was as clear in his head as if they were skateboarding together side-by-side, *'Yesss! Now balance and roll away!'*

Rox chanted, "TIM-MEE! TIM-MEE!" and soon they were all doing it.

Tim looked back at the football. He must have cleared it but he couldn't remember the jump at all. It didn't matter. He was exultant. He let the board drift, ran back and sent the football in a long banana kick between the two school bins. Somebody threw him another ball and with his left heel, he flicked it high and headed it into the same goal. Roaring with pleasure, Tim ran around the playground, his arms wide in victory.

He didn't get far. Rox shouted, "Behind you", just as somebody large lifted him off the ground.

"You snotrag! This time you're dead!" Big Danny yelled.

Mrs Cox pushed through the crowd shouting, "Boys!"

Tim dared to open his eyes. Mrs Cox was standing glaring at them. Danny let him go. *Not again*, Tim thought, *more detention*. He felt in his pocket for Grandpa's spanner. It wasn't there.

"I told you, Mrs Cox, didn't I?" Rox said, pushing to the front.

"You did, Roxanne. I should have known it was Daniel's lot causing trouble, not Tim. I have a treat for you, Daniel. I want you to clean out the boys' toilets."

"With his tongue?" offered Rox.

"Not quite. With his friends though, I think. And Tim," she said, beaming at Tim, "I had no idea you were such a talented footballer. See me tomorrow, first break. Now, to the toilets, you lot."

As Big Danny and his gang slouched away, Tim searched his pockets. He ran after them.

"Give me my glasses back," he demanded.

Miserably Danny handed them over.

"And the spanner."

"Whah . . ." Danny said. It wasn't a question.

"You got my spanner. My skate tool."

"Nah," Danny spat and followed Mrs Cox.

"You have so!" Tim shouted, but the crowd was round him, whacking him on the back, and he couldn't follow.

Rox touched his shoulder. "Pete's sister told me Pete was boasting about beating you up. I was right to tell, wasn't I?" she asked.

She sounded really worried, in case she'd got it wrong.

Tim gave her a smile. "Yeah. I'm glad you did. Thanks."

"You were brilliant," she smiled back.

Suddenly Tim realised what had happened. He punched the air.

"I *won!*" he yelled. He couldn't wait to get home and tell Mum.

* * *

"Tim?" Rox was tapping his door. "She wasn't listening properly."

"Go away."

Tim was guiding his mouse with the utmost skill, blasting away on Killer III. To Tim each monster was his darling mother who had completely misunderstood his great victory and assumed — how could she? — that he *Tim* had picked a fight with Big Danny and that he *Tim* had been punished.

"She was on the phone to her agent and didn't hear properly."

"I don't care."

Kerpaff! Egg yellow blood all over the screen!

Rox was standing, in her irritating way, looking over his shoulder. "That's *gross*," she said. He knew what was coming next.

"Ti-im — can I have a go?"

Why did she always do that? The minute he got onto a new level for the first time, she appeared from nowhere and demanded a go. Say no, and it was tantrum time. But Tim had been pushed around enough.

"NO WAY!!!" he yelled.

More Killer III monsters exploded in yellow pulp. His score was going to be incredible.

"Who's that?" Rox asked. "That face?"

Tim leant back and half-closed his eyes. Killer III had no faces in it.

142

"It's looking at me," Rox said.

"What?"

"Get the WYSIWYG file, Tim. Look! It's the worst yet!"

"WYSIWYG's gone, remember," Tim said. He still hadn't told her about WYSIWYG 2. There was no point now he had deleted all its contents.

Rox sat down beside him. This was always bad news. She peeled his hand firmly off the mouse. He was helpless. Bellowing about losing his best ever score made no difference as Rox swivelled the mouse, scrolled up and down, double click and . . . she was into WYSIWYG 2. They both nearly choked.

The screen was full of writing:

Pride goeth before destruction and a haughty spirit before a fall. ADMIT IT!

Rox scratched her head, more frightened then she wanted to show.

"I know who can sort this out," she said, "Mrs Baldock. I'm going to get her!"

Tim didn't dare touch the mouse. For the first time in his life, Rox could be right.

Rox flew round to Mrs Baldock's flat. She was so terrified that Mrs Baldock couldn't understand her at first.

"No," Rox stuttered. "I said screen, not scream, though I screamed as well."

"Whatever this is," Mrs Baldock said calmly, "if it's sending messages our job's half done. It means it wants to meet us."

Mrs Baldock fetched her suitcase and in no time she was meandering through the Exworths' flat going, "No, no, maybe . . ." until she and Rox reached Tim's room. He was still staring at the laptop.

"I asked your Gran to leave out a bowl of water," Mrs Baldock said. "Any idea where she put it? Ah!"

She suddenly charged into the chapel, the suitcase swinging, "Here we are!"

Tim and Rox followed.

Mrs Baldock sniffed her pink plastic bowl, held it up to the stained glass light in cupped hands and swirled it clockwise, then anti-clockwise.

"We've got action in here all right," she whispered.

"What sort of action?" Rox asked, rubbing her arms against the cold.

"Not sure. What did your psychic friend think?"

"He took fright and scarpered," Tim muttered. It didn't seem so funny now.

"Typical!" Mrs Baldock's voice echoed along the vaulted ceiling, "Psychic experts aren't what they were."

"What you see isn't what you get?" Tim ventured.

"If you mean are people always what they say they are, then no. We know that. For instance, whoever kidnapped Rox and Georgie wasn't me. Nothing like me. Now what are we going to do? Any suggestions?"

Tim and Rox looked down at their feet.

"We hoped you would know, Mrs B," Tim murmured.

"I'll look up my books and let you know this evening. But this seems to be where it's centred. Here in this chapel. Definitely."

They followed Mrs Baldock back down the spiral staircase.

"What's centred?" Rox asked.

"Your paranormals. Nasty paranormals they are too."

"What paranormals?" Tim asked, pretty sure he wouldn't like the answer.

"You tell me, you activated them."

"Me?" Tim and Rox shouted together.

Mrs Baldock bit her pipe. "I told you before, Rox. You two have awakened all this. I can feel it off you."

"Is it out to kill us?" Rox groaned.

"Could be."

"What if we don't believe in ghosts?" Tim asked, still hoping for a sensible explanation.

Mrs Baldock stopped and touched his cheek. "You know, Tim," she said, "you of all people."

"Know what?" he asked but Mrs Baldock just handed the bowl of water to Rox and bustled away.

"No rest for the wicked," she said as she left, "I've got more Henrys due any minute. See you this evening."

Tim followed Rox into the kitchen where she was scrubbing Mrs Baldock's bowl as though it was poisonous. He wanted to say something. Ask something. Did Mrs Baldock still think he was psychic? She'd said so once. But where would he start? It was time he got on with his homework anyway. Which reminded him that he had to see Mrs Cox tomorrow. She'd been smiling when she said it, so for once it could be good news.

145

Chapter Twenty-Two

Tim had just had the best Friday of his life. Not only had he had a whole day free of grief from Big Danny, but, he had seen Mrs Cox at first break and, yes, yes, yes! — he was in the First Team. Starting next day. He didn't care anymore that a ghost was maybe trying to kill him!

Not that anybody was there to tell when he got home. Mum was out auditioning for a new role and wasn't back yet. He wasn't talking to her anyway — not after yesterday.

The sitting room door was shut, which meant Dad could be in there with another exorcist. Tim put his ear to the keyhole and had just identified the mystery guest when Georgie slid across the hall to show Tim his loose tooth.

"Ugh!" Tim shouted, suitably revolted. "Come and stick your tongue out, look just through this door here. I'll open it for you."

"How will that help?" asked Georgie, bowing to Tim's superior knowledge in tooth matters.

"It won't but Mr MacFadyen's in the sitting room and I don't like him."

"Gran does," Georgie said, "so I do too." Tim edged the door open but Georgie marched straight in.

Dad and Mr MacFadyen were chatting in armchairs by the fire. Tim pushed past Georgie and said, "I'm in the First Team, Dad. From tomorrow."

"Excellent," Dad said and pranced around an imaginary ball. As if this wasn't embarrassing enough, Gran then swept in. Tim hadn't confessed to her yet that he had lost Grandpa's precious spanner. Fortunately Gran was concentrating on her tray.

"I'm in the First Team, Gran," Tim said.

"Lovely, darling," she said. Tim noticed that she poured the tea with a flourish and was very keen to make sure that Mr MacFayden had exactly the right amount of milk. What was she up to?

"You won't mind if Fuschia, I mean Mrs Baldock, drops in for a moment?" Gran asked Dad, pressing Mr MacFadyen to have another biscuit. "She wants to do some sweeping up."

"What's that woman doing our cleaning for?" Dad snorted.

"You'll see," Gran said and winked at Tim.

He grinned back. Mrs Baldock must have come up with a plan to get rid of their paranormals.

The old witch trudged in. Without looking at the men, she raised her sword high above her head with both hands and chanted:

"O magick herbs of root and flower,
  Give this sabre healing power!"

Tim and Georgie nudged each other.

"Look, I'm sorry, Mrs Baldock," Dad cut in. "We're having a meeting in here."

Mrs Baldock was undaunted.

"Let all evil presence flee where'er it strikes! So mote it be! Where's the water, Dora?" she asked.

147

Gran bustled off to fetch the water bowl. Mrs Baldock adjusted its position on the mantelpiece, muttered again and went out. Gran followed with a cheery byeee.

Tim and Georgie tiptoed after them.

"Wonderful woman your mother-in-law," Mr MacFadyen said, brushing a drop of tea from his moustache. "I'm not so sure about the other one."

"Mrs Baldock means well, but I think I liked it better when we weren't on speaking terms," Dad said. "Did I tell you I went window-shopping today? I bought twenty-*four* windows and the builder's coming to fit them next week. So, back to the big question – when can we break into the secret room?"

"Mr Exworth, there are forms to be filled in. Consents to be obtained. You can't go knocking things down in a building like this without going through procedures."

"WHY NOT?" Dad erupted. "It's nearly two weeks now since the children found it."

Mr MacFadyen stirred his tea ferociously.

"We've got to do it right," he said, "One step at a time. It's the only way."

*   *   *

Rox was up to her neck in bath water again. One spell at a time, she was thinking, as she listened to Mrs Baldock stamping outside on the landing. Mrs Baldock had made no promises but Rox had high hopes of this latest bout of 'sweeping up'. In fact it could be working already. The nightmares hadn't bothered her for two nights now and Rox felt so much better. Or maybe it was her own spell that made her feel that way? Her love spell? She dipped her hair and listened again.

She could hear Tim swanking all over the flat telling everybody that he'd been picked for the First Team. You would think it was important. Rox had her own piece of news. Not that she could tell anyone yet except . . .

Dear Hannah Heartfixer,

I was dead interested in Emma's letter last week. I know where she's coming from and I have the answer. All you need to get the deeply gorgeous hunk in question to love you is a red candle and the bones of a European vixen . . .

Rox watched two bubbles merge into one, smiled and murmured to herself, "Jack, you are mine. And the next time we're together, you will take off your T-shirt. That will mean you admit the truth — that *you* are my destined love."

Rox got dressed in her black pyjamas and black dressing gown and went downstairs to find Gran.

Georgie raced across the hall wiggling his tooth to make her sick, so she offered to yank it out for him.

"It doesn't hurt, come here, I'll show you," Rox smiled sweetly.

Georgie shrieked and ran into the kitchen with Rox chasing him. Gran and Mrs Baldock filed in a procession down the stairs and followed them.

Gran filled another plastic bowl with water and set it in the middle of the table. Mrs Baldock threw salt at it, missed and then started to whirl her sword around her head again. When she realised she might be pushed for space she dangled it instead. Georgie took his light sabre out of the broom cupboard and whirled that.

"*Ye venoms most foul now hearken to me . . .*" Mrs Baldock faltered, " *. . . to me . . .* Dora, what comes next?"

"Don't ask me, dear. Start again and see how you go," Gran said.

"It's okay, it's coming back to me now," Mrs Baldock sighed. She chanted:

"Ye venoms most foul, now hearken to me!
Depart forthwith and banished be.
Fly far hence and ne'er return,
Or in the pit of fire,
I'll damn ye to burn."

Mrs Baldock drew breath from the very core of her body, shouted, "*SO MOTE IT BE!*" and slumped in Dad's chair.

"Is Mrs Baldock all right?" Rox whispered to Gran.

Tim rushed in from the sitting room to see what all the noise was about.

"She's wrestling with venoms most foul," Gran said.

"Serves her right. She said it was all my fault. And Rox's," Tim snorted.

"What?" Gran whispered.

"All this," Tim said, "ghost stuff. But it's not our fault. It can't be."

Gran patted his hand, "Of course not, love."

150

Rox glanced at Mrs Baldock, "She looks flushed. Do you think the venoms most foul are listening?"

"I wouldn't want to say anything," Gran said, sucking her top teeth, "but I wonder if she's getting a bit past it."

Tim let that one go. "Did you hear, Rox," he grinned, "I've been picked for the First Eleven?"

"You've been shouting it all over the flat," Rox groaned. "Well done, though."

"I hear you've been a bit of a hero in other ways and all," Gran said and kissed his left ear.

Wiping it dry, Tim admitted that he had been in a bit of a scuffle, yes, and was about to say that Grandpa had seen him right when he stopped. Gran might ask him about Grandpa's spanner. He was pretty sure that Big Danny had taken it hostage but he had no proof and no way of getting it back.

Dad tapped the doorframe and stared at Mrs Baldock lolling in his chair.

"Mr MacFadyen's just going and wanted to say goodbye," he grimaced.

Mr MacFadyen was nodding so hard his head nearly fell off. He handed the tray to Gran, "This is such a charming flat and you really are a most charming lady."

"You love these old buildings, don't you?" Gran simpered.

"Oh, I do," he said, bobbing on his toes. "You could say my life is in ruins. I'm going to see what I can do for you all just as fast as I can."

He reached for Gran's hand and kissed it.

151

Gran was actually smiling back. Tim's face was hot with embarrassment. Even his dad was blushing.

A snore from Mrs Baldock broke the moment and everybody laughed, just as Mum came in.

"That's what I like," she said, "a big reaction from my audience." She shook rain from her coat, "Well? What have I missed?"

While Dad showed Mr MacFadyen out and Gran gently woke her friend, Rox tried to explain.

"There was this screen, thing on Tim's screen, and I screamed and Mrs Baldock came with her bowl and has been sweeping up and . . ."

"Slow down," Mum said, "and breathe." Mum breathed in slowly, and out again, with her hands splayed in front of her. The audition had done her good.

"Mrs Baldock's been doing another spell, and drinking wine, and she says all the ghost stuff is our fault, me and Rox," Tim said, not looking at Mum.

"So it's you two playing a joke, is it?" Dad asked fiercely, as he hung up Mum's coat in the hall. "Well, you can stop it right now, I've had this nonsense up to here!"

"It's not a joke, Dad!" Tim shouted. His perfect day was in pieces. "I don't *believe* in ghosts, I never have and I never will!"

"Tim," Mum said quietly. "I'm sorry I didn't listen to you properly yesterday. Rox told me what happened."

It's okay," Tim muttered, meeting her eyes. He grinned, "I'm in the First Team."

"Fantastic!" she said, gave him a hug.

Rox stamped out and up the stairs. If Tim mentioned the First Team once more, she'd be sick all over him.

At the top of the stairs she realised she was starving and stamped down again. "Are we having any dinner tonight or not?" she bellowed.

Mum started to fuss that they were all useless without her and was soon on the phone ordering pizzas.

"Mrs Baldock?" she called, "Rox go and find out what pizza Mrs Baldock wants, love."

Rox looked everywhere but there was no sign of Mrs Baldock downstairs. Perhaps she'd gone home to sleep. Rox was about to give up when she heard a groan from the stairs. The old woman was on her hands and knees near the top step, dragging herself up, as if each step took all her strength.

Rox rushed up to help her. The old witch's fingernails clawed at the stone as if somebody was trying to kill her. A deep voice rushed from Rox's mouth before she could stop it, "Admit IT!" It was the voice from her nightmares.

Rox froze with shock, then sat down on the step. She had to. She watched Mrs Baldock turn slowly to face her. But it wasn't the nice Mrs Baldock who had just been snoring downstairs. This Mrs Baldock's face was as pale as cheese, with eyes full of icy hatred.

Rox couldn't move. Then very, very slowly the eyes blinked, and turned into their Mrs Baldock's eyes again. Colour flooded the old woman's cheeks and she smiled.

"Hello, Rox, what you doing here? What am *I* doing here? What a funny place to fall asleep!"

Rox's heart was crashing and she wanted to cry. Nobody in the whole world would believe what had just happened. Except Mrs Baldock — the real Mrs Baldock. So she told her.

Mrs Baldock put an arm around her shoulder as Rox shivered and let the tears come.

"It's clever, this paranormal," the old woman said as she smoothed Rox's hair. "We're not through this yet, are we? Not by a long chalk."

Chapter Twenty-Three

Next morning while everybody else was busy having breakfast, Dad was pacing by the phone. The second the phone rang he grabbed it. "Yes. No. I suppose so. Thanks."

He banged down the receiver and turned around, enjoying the tension.

"What did he say?" Tim asked.

"MacFadyen's got us permission to break into the secret room, from the Secretary of State no less. He's emailing me a copy. And the builder says he might even condescend to come in person if we pay him first. But he can't come until — you'll never believe this — Friday week!"

"Friday week!" Rox shouted. "That's pathetic! We could all be dead by then!"

"We could be deaf by tonight," Mum said quietly, "if you don't stop shouting."

Rox stuck out her tongue.

"Can I help do the break-in?" Tim asked.

"Me too," Georgie said.

"No," Dad said, "far too dangerous. There'll be sledgehammers and all sorts."

"Pleease," Tim begged.

"No," Dad insisted. "It's adults only."

"Except for me," Mum said. "I'm staying well clear."

* * *

And me, Rox thought, as she lay in her bed that night. She spread her jet tassel on her throat. Another thirteen days meant another thirteen nights, which could mean another thirteen nightmares. Maybe she should go and sleep in Mum and Dad's room again? *No*, she thought, *if I lie here, I'll be all right*.

Her eyes started to shut.

. . . Admit IT!

"Oh no," she breathed and opened her eyes. Her heart was pounding again. She mustn't fall sleep. She'd stay awake all night, on vigil. "I will not let my eyelids drop . . . I will not!" she chanted.

Rox heard church bells in the distance chime ten and later eleven times. She would not fall sleep. If only she wasn't so exhausted . . .

. . . hear the sounds of the night, the echoes of fright and the breeze in the trees. I watched you crawl up here, panting on every step, hauling your broken body along the landing to the Sacristy door. 'Admit it,' I said, as you slumped inside. I can wait, in my hate. I will watch you, curled on this floor. You will not escape. You will sweat and fret, within the net I set for you.

Rox sat up, wide awake, clutching her jet beads. Get out of my mind, she begged, you horrible nightmare, get out! Reading was the answer. She reached down beside her bed and found the *Horrendous Hamper of Horrible Ghost Stories, Volume III*. Well, that was no help. She felt further under the bed and lifted out *Illuminated Letters*, a book she was supposed to have read for Art homework. She thought she had lost it but here it was, a beautiful book. It was the words she loved best: gouache and tempera, ultramarine, Prussian blue, lapis lazuli, burnt umber . . . This would definitely keep her awake. Yes, these gorgeous words . . .

. . . *from the very day you arrived, you annoyed me. I had never clapped eyes on anyone so pompous, so puffed full of his needs, for inks of the finest quality and the most expensive vellum. 'How could you honour the Abbey with less than the best reeds and quills?' you said.*

But the nicest cell was too good for you. You had to sleep in the chapel, by the altar. On the icy floor. On your second day you announced that that was no good. 'Weren't you comfortable in the chapel?' we asked. 'That is the problem,' you said, 'too comfort-able.' You moved into the little sacristy where you could not stretch your full length. 'Could our dear Lord stretch his legs on the Cross?' you said. So arrogant. Can you stretch now, Brother Scribe? Can you stretch your broken bones?

Go on, scratch your way out. Yes, I hear you. Could our Lord scratch his way off the Cross? They have all forsaken you, you know. We are alone. I hear . . . silence. Why have you stopped groaning? I need a candle. Quick, I will fetch a candle from the chapel.

You're so small in your rags. Your shoulders feel like sticks. And your eyes, they're open as if you're alive. My candle flame glints in them, like life. No! Not yet! You must not die yet, Brother Scribe. You must admit it first. You must not die before you admit your pride! Admit it!

I crouch and take your inky fingers in mine. Could this be victory? You have not spoken and will never speak again. I am overwhelmed with woe. You made me do this, you made me feel this hate. I only wanted to feed you and you made me wish you dead.

They will find us soon, I know. I must die too. Like this candle flame I must. Lord, Lord, all my life I have longed to reach you, hold you, but I could no more hold you close to me, Lord, than I can wrap my fingers round this flame and squeeze it. My . . . aaah! My sleeve burns. My habit too. Lord, agony is searing my body, it is right, this torment. Take me, Lord, take me, deliver me from this soulless victory . . .

Rox sat up panting on the edge of her bed. Her arms and legs felt full of red-hot pins. She tried to scream but no sound would come. Within a few seconds, an eternity, the pain faded and blood flowed back into her veins.

She wasn't sure how much more of this she could take.

*   *   *

Tim's mind was in hyper-race. He had been lying awake too, thinking about another thirteen nights. It would be good to get into the secret room at last. Maybe there *was* something in there that would make sense of what was happening. Rox had been quiet all day, too quiet. He had caught Mrs Baldock giving her a hug when she came back from school. He wished she wouldn't do that. Mrs Baldock's spells just made things worse. If everybody would just forget about the whole ghost business it would probably stop.

The trouble was, every time Tim wasn't thinking about the ghost, he found himself going back over his latest brush with Big Danny. It hadn't taken long for Danny to get back to hassling him. Tim couldn't help reliving the clump, clump of Big Danny's boots following him up the corridor that morning. Then that whisper, hot and moist in his ear, as Danny jostled him on the way into assembly.

"Where's your spanner, Timmy?" Danny hissed.

"You tell me," Tim whispered back. If he didn't whisper he'd get told off for talking.

"Me?" Danny said and kicked Tim's ankle, as if by accident.

Mrs Cox had spotted it, wonders will never cease, and confiscated Danny's boots, so he had to spend the whole day in his socks. Danny was hardly likely to let Tim forget that.

An internal twinge suggested a visit to the loo. How dare Big Danny torment him even in his sleep? He headed for the bathroom.

The daytime rumpus – planes, sirens, the distant chink of dishes – was all horribly missing. Even his tread on the carpet was more silent than usual. On his way back to his bedroom something creaked. Tim felt the bobbly wallpaper for comfort. Was it Tim himself or something else? What if it were some*one* else? Tim whipped round and saw – nothing just darkness as dark as closed eyes.

He could hear someone though. Breathing.

"Who's that?"

"Me."

Tim had never been so pleased to hear her voice. "Rox! What are you doing up?" he whispered.

Careful not to wake anybody, Rox hissed, "I couldn't sleep. Nightmares."

Tim did not dare say that Big Danny had been chasing him in his dreams too.

"I think I know what the haunting is all about," she whispered, poking him on the shoulder.

"Yeah, yeah," Tim broke in, but she ignored him,

"Listen! Somebody used to live here and I think he killed somebody."

"How do you know?" Tim whispered.

"In this dream I had."

"A *dream*." Even Rox couldn't take a *dream* seriously.

"No," her voice grew panicky, "it was real. He thought it was a victory but it wasn't and he burned himself." She took a deep breath, "It's the ghost."

"Don't be stupid, there's no ghost," Tim whispered. "I'm going back to bed."

"Don't Tim. Don't leave me!"

She sniffed, more upset than Tim had realised.

"You were dreaming!" Tim hissed. "That's all."

"Dream this then." Rox said, slapping him. It was not a playful slap. It was not a coy, 'let's play cops and drug barons and I'll run away before you can get me back' sort of slap. She had been building up to this all his life.

Tim gasped and slapped her back. She shoved him hard against the banister as if she was trying, with all her strength, to push him over the edge.

From somewhere in the cold, dark air around them came a faint gasping sound. It was as if somebody was heaving himself up the stairs in the dark with his dying breath. Outside the trees suddenly rustled in the wind, and the chapel door opened and slammed shut.

Rox bolted straight down the corridor to Mum and Dad's room.

Tim stood alone on the landing. He had heard it this time. His knees felt as if they had been replaced with wool but he managed to feel his way along the bobbly wallpaper to the chapel.

As he turned the door handle he knew that if he was ever going to find out what was going on, it had to be now.

Chapter Twenty-Four

Grandpa's whisper was so real, Tim could almost touch it, *"You can do it."*

"Do what?" he muttered.

A crack jagged across the chapel wall. Dust peppered the floor.

"You mean bust it down?" Tim shouted. A crack streaked across Mum's yellow blotches. Tim could taste his own fear.

"But . . . I CAN'T!"

"Go on," Grandpa whispered behind him. A pot of paint rolled and stopped at Tim's feet. Tim slung it at the wall and yellow splashed everywhere. Nothing happened.

"Go on," Grandpa said again.

Tim grabbed two more pots, took a huge breath and closed his eyes. He ran full pelt at the wall. The wall crumbled and caved away.

Tim flew inside, head first, over a heap of bricks. He had time to be aware of smoke stinging his eyes and then his throat was swelling up, as sturdy hands grabbed him. He was pulled along and dumped in a corner of a narrow room with one small arched window. Someone was standing over him, holding a candle. It was someone who hadn't had a bath in quite a while.

"Stay there," it growled.

Not Grandpa, that was for sure, but he had heard that voice before.

Tim curled up, numb with terror. It was as if evil was wrapping itself around him. It was so tight he could hardly breathe. Tim peered through his fingers and saw a figure standing in front of him. It looked like a picture he'd seen a few times in the school bible, with these three guys called Shadrach, Meshach and Abednego in it. He had often wondered about those guys. They'd been strolling through the flames in their floor-length robes, hands clasped behind them, with their hooded heads bowed.

The figure in front of Tim was not so relaxed. Its hood was so big that he couldn't see a face. Hands, wrapped around a thick church candle, jutted out from the loose sleeves. The flame quivered as the figure bent closer to Tim. Something about the hooded monk glowed with a silent promise to do Tim incalculable harm.

Tim felt anger bubbling up. He'd taken on Big Danny and lived. Was he going to be scared every day of his life or was he going to fight back now too?

"Oh that's dead brave!" he sat up and shouted through clenched teeth. "You're nothing but a bully!"

He had to escape. All he had to do was go back the way he'd come, back to the chapel and run. He crawled backwards, his heart hammering, and felt behind him. But the wall was solid again. The more he pushed, the more solid it felt. There had to be a way through. He hammered till his hands were stinging.

Well, that did it. He was *sure* he was dreaming now. If only he could stop dreaming that evil smell.

The figure stretched its skinny fingers toward Tim's face as though it was going to stroke his cheek. Ragged nails dug into Tim's chin.

"OW! Get off," Tim shouted.

This was the worst dream Tim had ever had and he'd had enough of it.

"You don't frighten me," he yelled. The fingers thrust away Tim's face as if he were dirt. Out in the corridor Tim could hear people jostling and talking. Above it all was his dad's voice, "What are you standing there for? Give me that sledgehammer!"

Tim stood up and called, "Help!"

The creature stepped closer, clasped Tim's throat in one hand and started to squeeze. Tim felt his blood pulsing like thunder. Darkness flickered at the edges of his eyes, then more darkness and more, as if he might never see again.

"I was six when I came here," the monk said.

Tim tried to shout but his throat felt as if it was full of spiders.

"I remember it so well," the ghost whispered, tightening his grip, "tall men talking far above my head. And when my mother left me – left me without a single look – Father Abbas said to me, 'Idleness is the enemy of the soul.'"

The hand loosened slightly at the word 'soul'. Tim just had time to feel he might not die that very minute, before the hand jerked tighter again.

"In the sweat of thy face," it went on, "shalt thou eat bread." The hand jerked again. "Genesis 3, 19. In the sweat of the baking it, more like. You understand the value of bread when you know the toil of its making. These hands . . . "

The monk's fingers dropped from Tim's neck. Tim fell to the floor, coughing. The monk spread his hands and stared at them. "These hands sieved a 1000 pounds of flour, in temperatures that would roast beef - wheaten, soda, raisin, plain."

Tim was nearly deafened by his own blood crashing in his ears. In the corridor outside he heard Dad grunt as he lifted something. Relief surged over Tim. He felt his way, on his hands and knees, towards that grunt, "Dad? Dad!" But the monk moved and Tim was staring at the creature's sandaled feet.

"Four hours on the hot bread line every day before breakfast!" it said. The ghoul began to pace. Tim couldn't get past. "Wheaten, soda, raisin, plain," it was ranting now, "the way of sanctity, the staff of life!"

The monk stopped, pulled Tim to his feet and bellowed, "ADMIT IT!"

Tim could have touched the creature's hood to see if it felt real, but his arms were pinned. He peered into the folds, looking for a face or a single feature. Nothing. Tim yelled, "Come *on*, Dad! Why aren't you here yet? Why?"

"Why?" the monk roared and raised the candle to the ceiling. The echo bounced along the ribbed arches. "Why did you come back? You must admit it!"

"What are you on about?" Tim screamed. "Admit WHAT?"

The monk started pacing again, "You with your bed of stone and your endless fasting. Why did you do that? Why? Isn't why the biggest question in the universe? Bigger than the four corners of the flat Earth?"

Beads of sweat poured down Tim's back. Why was he trapped with this faceless horror, who knew nothing about basic cosmology? His heart was still crashing with fear but it seemed to speed up his thinking, as if everything else was in slow motion.

"The Earth doesn't have any corners," he croaked. "Don't you know that?"

The monk stopped. "Ha!" it roared. "Heresy too."

"Everybody knows the Earth is round," Tim ventured. He stepped closer to the monk. "What about if I prove it to you? Have you ever seen an eclipse?"

The ghost shuddered.

"Of course," it snapped, "you of all people know that!"

"Who do you mean, who is this You?" Tim begged.

"Father Abbas ordered us all to be on the lawn at midnight and there we all stood watching the moon go pink, witnessing the miracle when Father Abbas noticed you were missing! I offered to go and find you." The ghost spread the fingers of its free hand and stared at them. "I had been greasing loaf tins all day but I found the strength to haul you from your bed and throw you on the floor. And what did you do, when you should have been grateful? You whined about the lard on my fingers."

Tim remembered with a jolt where he'd seen those hands before, wringing in front of his face in his own bedroom.

"Father Abbas authorised the lard!" the monk spat. "But that did not suit you. Oh no"

"Nothing to do with me," Tim cut in, amazed that his voice could sound so casual. His legs were about to give way. His own hands were shaking and his stomach had folded up inside him as if it, for one, was out of there.

"Yes, YOU!" the monk yelled. "'This bread is too rich,' you said. 'Less mortification of the flesh is less given to God. Down what slope are we sliding, Brothers? It's the slope to Hell.' But I reminded you, that pride is the sin of the fallen angels and it grows so easily in virtue. 'The Archangel Gabriel visited me in a dream,' you whispered, 'and said lo, the way of the Lord is to eat less every day.' Could you not see that was Satan in angel's guise?"

The monk advanced on Tim.

"That's why I did it. For your sake! Pride had you in its grip," it snarled and the bony fingers jabbed Tim's chest. "I did it, yes, I painted bread rolls in your manuscripts, little loaves to tempt you, and did I get any thanks? None – you tried to throw me down the stairs." The figure jabbed Tim's chest again. Tim felt himself staggering, off-balance. He had no strength left in his legs, but if he fell, would he be able to get up again?

"But these baker's arms are stronger than your puny artist's hands . . ." the creature stopped. It sighed suddenly and swung away, sleeves billowing. "Wheaten, soda, raisin, plain," it said with a sob in its voice.

Tim took a huge breath and felt steadier, though no less afraid. "So did you see the eclipse or not?" he asked.

The monk turned slowly, as if every bone crackled with pain.

"Well?" Tim asked.

The monk put up a scrawny hand in self-defence.

"If you'd looked . . ." Tim said.

"No, no!"

"If you'd looked," Tim went on, "you'd have seen the Earth's shadow covering up the moon. Like somebody taking bites out of a biscuit because the shadow's round."

"Heresy!" the monk hissed. "Dangerous heresy. And there's only one cure for heresy . . . "

The monk held the candle aloft — "You too must burn in the pit of fire!" — and hurled the candle to the floor. Somehow the candle stayed lit as it rolled away and then rolled back under the monk's hem. Fire began to crackle as the creature grabbed Tim's throat again. Tim was shaking so much he could hear his own teeth rattling. He couldn't stand this nightmare a minute longer. Where was Grandpa when he needed him?

Tim put his hand up to his nose and squeezed. "Dere, dat's better," he muttered. Smoke was thickening around them both. Tim refused to breathe. One way or the other he'd find out now what was real.

Chapter Twenty-Five

The harder Tim held his nose, the more his eyes bulged, so he shut them to concentrate. His chest was sending fierce messages that air must come in. He counted to keep the pain away but by the time he reached forty he felt sick and faint. But he managed to hold on.

When he finally took a breath, he could feel a mixture of a sneeze and a force ten gale coming, "Whey-HOO!!!"

The spectre reeled back several feet, losing its grip on Tim's pyjamas. "That, my friend, is your last mortal act," he growled. "Unless . . . I take the girl instead!"

Later Tim hardly dared admit it — even to himself — but he gave the matter a moment's serious thought. Here was a way out of this torment, why shouldn't he take it? The noises out in the corridor had stopped. Had Dad and his help squad gone away? Even toe-to-toe with Big Danny, Tim had never felt so terrified and alone. And what did the monk mean by Take? Take where? Why?

Then he heard something. It sounded like Grandpa's cough. He could almost feel the old man tousling his head the way he used to. Sense dawned on him. This was *his* dream, not Rox's. If anything important was going to happen, it should happen to him, not Rox. Besides, if the figure were real, it wouldn't think twice about taking them both, and Georgie. Whatever deal he struck.

Tim took a deep breath.

"No, take me," he said, "but on one condition . . . "

"Condition?" the monk boomed. "You think you are in a position to negotiate? Ha!"

"Prove that the world has corners," Tim said, "and I'll come quietly."

"Prove to me it has not."

"Well . . . the Earth goes round the sun, the moon goes round the Earth and sometimes the Earth gets in between the other two, the moon and the sun . . . "

"HOLD!" the ghoul shouted, stepping closer, smoke seeping around his habit. Both hands twisted powerfully around Tim's upper arms and the ghost began to shake him to and fro, "Did not the saints live and die knowing that Our Lord's blessed, flat Earth was the centre of His Creation?"

Tim's brains were flopping painfully inside his head like soup.

"What was good enough for the saints is good enough for us," the monk hissed. "Use your eyes, boy! Trust your eyes! See the beauty of the Lord's flat horizon as the sea blends into the sky in the same FLAT shimmering blue!"

But the monk had seen part of an eclipse, a lunar one. What did he make of if? Tim was about to ask when the monk's fingers bit deeper into his shoulders.

"Come!" the monk said. "We are wasting time! We dare not escape our punishment."

170

The sledgehammer crashed against the wall like thunder. Help *was* coming.

"No, wait!" Tim shouted. Surely all he had to do was keep talking until Dad broke in. Which had better be quick. Smoke was stinging his eyes.

"Remember what I said about the eclipse?" he said. "There's something else, listen, in an eclipse you can see the Earth's shadow and it's round, remember? You see it moving, bit-by-bit, over the moon. Let me go a minute and I'll show you!"

The monk let go. If there had been somewhere to run to, Tim would have run for his life, but there wasn't. So he steadied his breath the best he could and croaked, "Watch this."

He swung one hand slowly from the left and the other from the right.

"They move round each other like this, see? And here's the really great bit," Tim said, lining his hands up in front of the ghost, "the Earth's shadow here" — he waggled his right hand — "and the moon here," he said waggling his left hand. "When you look at them from here on Earth, the sun and the moon, they're *exactly* the same size! See?"

There was a pause a person could drop to his death through. Tim breathed through his sleeve as the smoke thickened. He heard — was it possible — sobbing.

"I *see*," the creature was weeping. Its hands were working in front of it like Tim's, passing into alignment and out again. "I see . . . what I *see* . . . is the genius of our Creator! Stand amazed, heretic, stand amazed that everything our eyes can behold is but a speck on His fingertip. Our sun and stars are his playthings, the merest pretty baubles in the Heavens."

Tim heard a thud as the monk fell to its knees and Tim felt a twinge of something extraordinary inside him. He felt pity.

"Merciful Lord," the hooded monk said. "I know humility at last. You know I meant no harm! But how was I to know my little rolls and loaves would goad him so much?"

Another massive sledgehammer blow shuddered the wall. The monk lurched at Tim's arm.

Tim dodged away asking, "What happened? Did you fight him?"

The monk raised both shrivelled palms in the air:

"He came at me like a thousand bulls! The rage in his eyes as he fell over the banister. I never meant that. But he knew how to make me pay. In his death he suffered more. But what is that, Lord, compared with my torment? Wheaten, soda, raisin, plain . . . wretch that I am, forgive me Lord. Cleanse me with refining fire, this agony of flame. Let me burn with peace and joy, tears of joy. Aaaaah!"

The monk shuddered from the top of his hood to the floor and roared at the ceiling. At the same time something shivered through Tim. A memory? Recognition of something? Wasn't it on the day of the eclipse, when they were moving into the abbey, that time he and Rox were on the stairs? Tim was desperate not to fall over the banisters. He was caught up in overwhelming emotions, that ferocious need to survive. He had roared that day when he and Rox had fought just as the monks had done. Mrs Baldock had told them they had triggered all this. Could that be what she meant? Was that what the monk meant when he kept saying 'Admit it!'? Was he just talking to his victim or did he want him and Rox to admit their part in reawakening his hell?

A colossal sledgehammer blow to the wall almost stopped Tim's heart dead, it was so close. Dad would be through soon.

At the same moment the first shaft of morning sunshine struck through the stained glass window and sprinkled colours all over the monk's robe. The hooded head bowed. Gnarled fingers pulled at the habit, pushing and plucking at the bristly woollen cloth. The creature writhed and twisted in the smoke grunting with fury as if his flesh was burning, as if the habit itself was tearing at him.

The sledgehammer boomed again.

The monk flung back his hood and stood still. For two whole seconds Tim's heart stopped, then gave three beats together very fast before settling to the usual gallop. Above the monk's shoulders, where there should have been a head, shafts of rainbow light shone straight through.

Fear twisted Tim's stomach. Where was its head?

The monk bent double again, wrestling with the habit. The chipped nails ripped at the cloth on the shoulders and chest until suddenly the garment ripped down the middle and dropped to the floor.

Tim's heart felt as though it was going to burst. He could see clear through to the flames beyond. Where the monk should have stood exposed from head-to-toe, visible in some form at last, there was nothing.

173

Chapter Twenty-Six

"It was there, Dad," Tim whispered, "right where you are now."

"What, son?"

"The ghost, Dad. The GHOST!"

Dad smoothed wet hair off Tim's temples. "It's all right, son, let me look at your pupils."

Mrs Baldock was stamping and spinning on the landing, her nightie trailing under her coat.

"You've done it, lad," she roared. "You've got rid of him!"

"I feel as if I've run a marathon," Tim said, "twice."

Dad smoothed both his hands back over his bald patch and said, "Some dreams *are* hard work."

"You don't believe me?"

"Well . . . we thought Rox was doing her usual, with the dreams, but she made us come and check the chapel before she could sleep and . . . Tim, we *all* felt the heat! That's why we got the fire brigade. But there's no fire, no sign of one now. Was there a real fire? I mean . . . I . . . I don't believe in ghosts, Tim. And neither do you. You're my cast-iron scientific sceptic," Dad was panting. "What's going on?"

He wrapped his arms tighter around Tim until they both stopped trembling. Tim wished the hug would never stop. Dad's arms round him were just what he needed now. Mum could join in too, and Georgie and Gran. Even Rox.

But Rox could stand Tim being centre of attention only so long. How come he got hugs after a nightmare and all they did for her was laugh? *She'd* been the one who'd run to tell Mum and Dad. *She'd* shown everybody where the hidden door should be on the landing from the day she and Georgie had been kidnapped. Now Tim was getting all the attention because of a fire that wasn't even there. Worst of all, Tim said there was a ghost and they all believed him!

Dad had asked the fire chief how come they could all feel the heat when there was no fire? The fire chief had said it happens more often than you'd think and were there any young teenagers in the flat? Then they'd turned round and looked at Rox! As if it was all her fault!

The last thing she wanted was to agree with Tim but she *had* heard the chapel door open and close by itself. She'd been wide-awake talking to Tim.

She was far too tired to work it out. Mum was busy pounding about the flat checking everybody and waking Georgie up in the process. Dad was still gushing over Tim, and Gran and Mrs Baldock were in the kitchen going on about how wonderful Tim had been. The last place she would get any sleep was her own bed so she trudged back to Mum and Dad's.

Rox pulled the duvet up to her nose and was breathing in Mum's lovely warm bed smell when she heard it. Scratching. Right overhead. She was awake and she could hear scratching.

Mum and Dad came in with the boys, announcing that everyone was to sleep in the one room again, just this once.

Rox moved over to the camp bed but before she closed her eyes, she made a decision. As soon as it was light, she would call Jack. He was the very person — sensible, objective, and he'd never mentioned ghosts once — to climb into the attic and check for rats.

*　*　*

Jack didn't return her message until the Monday morning but once Rox explained the problem, he said he could fit in a quick visit later that afternoon. Would four-ish do? Perfect, she'd just be back from school.

All through Sunday everyone had been quiet, as if what had happened was too big to talk about. Mum was happy to pay Jack to come as long as he didn't cost too much. Rox had used the 'you never know, it might solve something' approach.

He was late of course. Four-ish turned out to be after five o'clock so Mum was busy cooking when Rox led him to the chapel. The trapdoor up to the attic was so stiff he had to force it open. Red-faced with effort, Jack winked at Rox and said, "Getting warm. Can't have that."

He peeled off his Muse T-shirt.

Rox felt her mouth drop open in astonishment as he exposed his thin, hairless chest. The stepladder creaked as he disappeared into the rectangular hole.

Rox did a jerky stamping dance of glee:

"He took his T-shirt off! He loves me!" she laughed. "He *loves* me! I can't wait to tell him how much I love him too!"

She heard him stepping carefully over the joists, then whispering and making kissing noises. What on earth was he up to? Jack's feet dangled back into view and he landed on the floor, puffing slightly. Cupped in one hand was a thin, sad-looking, three-inch long mouse.

"You wanna stroke him?" Jack asked.

Rox edged away.

Jack moved closer: "He's a shy little fella. Look," he said.

Rox finally looked. The mouse's black eyes met hers. *At least,* Rox thought, *with a mouse what you see is what you get — a mouse.* It must have nibbled its way over from Mrs Baldock's place.

Jack gently pinched the creature's tail, lifted its little face up to his own and made slurping, kissing noises at it. The mouse responded by exposing two long, very yellow front teeth.

"Better see if he's got any family," Jack said. "Five litters a year these little chaps have, up to twenty young each time."

Rox wished she could snap her nostrils shut like a seal under water. The mouse stank!

"He's really skinny," she managed to say.

"He's a house mouse. Doesn't look much, does he. You'd think he'd break like glass. But they're tough. They can live in Antarctica. They turn up inside shop fridges, all glossy, having the time of their lives," Jack said. "Some of them have even gone into space in rockets. Don't underestimate this little fella. They came from the Asiatic Steppes in somebody's handbag a few thousand years ago, and we've been living with them ever since."

Despite her revulsion, Rox was impressed.

Jack moved even closer. "He's lovely. Stroke him and you'll see". Before Rox could stop him, he had taken her finger and drawn it slowly down the mouse's backbone, link by clammy link. The fur was all loose, as if her finger could pull it off in pieces. Thinking that she might have preferred to be introduced to the ghost, Rox jerked her hand away.

"No offence, love. She don't mean it." Jack was talking to the mouse. He turned to Rox, his eyes deep brown like cola and said, "Right. Must go."

Must you, Rox thought. *Must you?*

A car hooted outside at the front of the flat.

"Jack," Mum called. "Your friend's here."

Rox heard heels clicking across the hall.

"We're stuffed, darling, the car's died." A blonde girl in a very short dress and long, high-heeled boots was standing by the umbrellas.

"Close your mouth, Tony," Mum said.

He did.

Tim was watching from the stairs, and laughing at his Dad. The girl held the mouse meekly by the tail while Jack put his T-shirt back on.

"Battery flat?" Jack asked.

"How do I know?" the girl said. "What shape should it be?"

"Give us the keys. I'll have a look."

Jack wandered out to the yellow car which had exhausts like silver drainpipes. It clearly did not cross

Chapter Twenty-Seven

Mum banged down the phone in the kitchen.

"The British Museum said they were sending their expert round and he's not just late," she fumed, "he's lost. I suppose he can't read a map unless it's got big spaces on it marked 'Here Be Dragons'."

Mum had phoned the museum first thing Tuesday morning. There were celebrations all round that the expert could come that Friday – today.

But Rox was not celebrating. She was still stunned by what she'd seen on those vellum pages. The little bread rolls. That tiny cottage loaf. They were straight from her nightmares! Not that she'd had any nightmares since the weekend. She almost wished one would come so that she could check if she was right.

Almost. She knew what reaction she'd get if she told anybody. Same old Rox, same old fantasy world. So she said nothing. She needed to see what the Museum man said though. That could only help.

So when the phone rang an hour later, Rox answered it immediately. A voice apologised for being late, he would be with them any minute. It was a voice she thought she recognised.

Sure enough, when the doorbell rang, who was on the doorstep but Mr MacFadyen. He'd thought the British Museum had got the wrong man when they rang him, so he'd ignored their message at first.

"Recognised by the BM!" he twittered. "Me!"

As Mum spread the old pages out on the sitting room floor, the phone rang again. Mum looked at Rox. Rox blanked her. After the eighth ring Mum stamped out to the kitchen muttering that if it was about double-glazing again, there could be murder done.

Mr MacFadyen peered over his half-moon spectacles.

"I gather you found this piece of history, Tim?" he asked.

"We all did," Rox butted in. "Are they valuable?"

Mr MacFadyen explained that he'd have to consult his colleague who had excavated the abbey before it was sold.

"He's in Tibet at the moment, meditating," Mr MacFadyen said, "doing something useful for once. He did uncover abbey records going back to the fourteenth-century, but how he missed these I don't know. Beautiful specimens."

Gran arrived and sat on the sofa. Tim noticed that her lipstick was an unusually bright pink.

"And are they worth anything?" she asked.

Mr MacFadyen wheeled to look at her.

"How delightful to see you, dear lady," he said.

Gran actually got up and kissed his cheek. Rox turned to wink at Tim who'd put two fingers down his throat. But Mr MacFadyen didn't notice. He was showing Gran the pages as though she was the only person in the room.

"They're probably more interesting than valuable but I'll take them back, date the soot in the ink and so on. If you hold this up to the light you can see pin

182

holes where compasses went in to draw the arcs," he smiled. "Very authentic. And you can feel the imprint here . . ." he said, taking Gran's hand and running her fingers gently over the sheet, ". . . where he ruled his lines with a dry hard point. This yellow should be a mix called arsenic sulphide and the red dots will be lead."

Mr MacFadyen stopped. He was still holding Gran's hand. She didn't seem to mind. "Dangerous work if only they'd known," he went on.

"Why?" Rox asked, bending over the pages.

"Lead's a poison," Mr MacFadyen explained. "If it gets in your mouth. Every time they licked their fingers . . ." He drew a finger across his throat and Tim laughed.

"Doesn't he know a lot?" Gran whispered in Rox's ear.

"Gran," Rox scowled, "don't. Just don't."

Gran patted Rox's hand as if some day Rox would understand the mysteries of love too. Rox stalked off to her room. She had too much to think about and Mr MacFadyen hadn't made it any easier.

Tim was still watching Mr MacFadyen and Gran when Mum came back.

"That was Tony on the phone, on his way home," she said. "What's the news?"

Mr MacFadyen brought her up-to-date. "But I'll take these away for further checking," he turned to Gran and smiled. "If you don't mind."

Gran smiled back.

Mum raised one eyebrow, spun on her heel and headed back to the kitchen.

Mr MacFadyen shook Gran's hand and said, "I'm so looking forward to tomorrow evening, dear lady."

Tim could feel his eyebrows climbing almost to his hairline. What was this? As soon as she closed the door Gran turned to Tim.

"I've got a date," she announced, as if she'd won a gold medal. "Mr MacFadyen and I are going to the ballet."

Tim couldn't think what to say. Part of him was horrified. Grandpa loved the ballet. How could she go with somebody else? But she looked so happy.

"Does Mum know?" he asked.

"Not yet," Gran said, "but she will in a minute."

Gran went into the kitchen. About ten seconds later he heard a saucepan clatter to the floor and Mum shouting, "WHAT!"

Tim was taking cover in the sitting room when he spotted Mr MacFadyen's clipboard on his chair. The little man had been so busy smiling at Gran he'd forgotten it. Tim grabbed it and ran out just in time to see Mr MacFadyen's green Morris Minor rolling away through the gates.

"Your clipboard, Mr MacFadyen!" he shouted. "Your clipboard!"

But the car was gone. Dad came huffing up the hill on his way from the station.

"What you got there Tim?" he said. "Let's have a shufti." Soon he was grinning and turning page after page of Mr MacFadyen's confidential work.

"Well, well, well," he grinned. "Our friend Mac-Fadyen, expert in ancient buildings and so-called impeccable taste, has another job apart from bothering us. He runs a huge company called Aardvark Megabuild PLC. Who build – wait for it – skyscrapers!"

Tim whistled through his teeth and said, "Not quite what he seems." He didn't mention Gran's date. He'd leave that one to Mum.

"Let's see what he makes of this little trick," Dad said, marching into the house.

"Dad, don't," Tim shouted but Dad was already inside at his laptop typing an e-mail with something that looked like glee.

Chapter Twenty-Eight

Tim was gliding down the Avenue in Greenwich Park next day on his skateboard, casually doing ollies over manholes and talking to himself. He was about to play for the First Eleven for the first time. Even though there was no way he would be captain for ages, he couldn't help practising his speech:

"You can't bounce it or head it or pass it but it's the most valuable stuff in the world."

He started singing to the tune of Old MacDonald's Farm, "What you see's *not* what you get, ee - I - ee - I - oh!"

A rumble of skateboard thunder came from behind. Big Danny and his gang had arrived. Their faces were all painted chalk-white with huge, dark eyes.

"Say your prayers, Timmy Wimmy!" Big Danny said, "or sing them if you like. Either way, you die!" He punched Tim in the stomach.

Tim stumbled back off his board and sat with a bump on the path. Mist was rising inside him – a mist of rage. If he was late for football, he'd kill them.

In his pocket Tim fingered Rox's silver cross. He had an idea. He rose to his feet, grabbed his board and dangling the cross in his hand, circled Danny stamping and chanting:

"*Our flat was haunted by a monk.
I fought him and he did a bunk.*

Watch out in case I bite a chunk
from YOU!
You smelly heap of JUNK!"

"You say junk?" Danny called and slowly pulled from his own pocket, as Tim had suspected, Grandpa's spanner. It was battered, as if Danny's gang had been stamping on it.

"Give it back!" Tim yelled.

Danny held it high above Tim's head. "Fight you for it," he snarled.

Tim would have been happy to pulverise Danny and lie beside him in hospital gloating over the damage but Danny had other ideas.

"Knife!" he commanded.

Nobody moved.

He said it again, "Knife!"

Pitbull Pete reached inside his boot and was soon grinning at Tim over the point of a long rusty blade.

Danny took the knife and swung his arm in an arc so that the tip of the blade just missed Tim's chin. Then he yawned and ambled over to a bed of shrubs.

Tim could have run for it, then or at any time during the long minutes Danny took to fell a smallish holly bush. But they'd have caught him and anyway running wouldn't solve anything. As Danny hauled the bush across the path Tim reckoned it was over a foot high, excluding spikes.

Danny pulled Grandpa's spanner from his pocket and laid it on the ground beyond the bush. He lit a cigarette and surveyed the obstacle. He surveyed it some more, decided it was too easy and shifted the spanner further from the bush.

Danny blew smoke in Tim's face and hissed, "You first!"

How could Tim do it? Even if he made it over the holly, which was unlikely, he would be bound to land on the spanner. Things seem to be magnetic when you have to avoid them. It would never survive the blow. Grandpa's spanner, which Gran had hoarded for so long, wrapped in love, would be scrap metal and Danny's lot would still beat him up. What do I do, Grandpa? Just slink away?

Grandpa whispered inside his head, *"Breathe, Tim. Breathe and think."*

Tim's anger pumped through his veins and he felt a strength that was not just his own. Before he really planned to, he was rushing at Danny. They went over together, sliding and squelching in the wet grass.

In a film these things happen smoothly, one punch, then the next. That's not what happened to Tim. His mind flipped back in terror to the last time he had thrown himself into an experience he would rather forget. But he had survived that and he would survive this too.

"You can do it," Grandpa whispered.

"All right, all right," was Tim's mumbled reply. He waded into the fight with his legs feeling heavy and his chest full of a terrible urge to cry. Danny's arms wrapped round him and Tim was being tossed right and left. Danny's laugh scorched his ears as Tim watched the clouds shoot suddenly to the left and his right cheek smashed on the ground. He was suddenly airborne again with his cheekbone stinging and his glasses skewed. The clouds zigged back into place. He tried to feel if there was blood.

"You can do it." Tim could almost feel Grandpa's tweedy hug. *"You can."*

With a mighty twist Tim's arm was free. His hand went up to fix his glasses and somehow in the muddle of this manoeuvre his elbow abruptly met flesh – Danny's flesh. Drizzle began to sprinkle Tim's face. Tim realised that his lower lip was bleeding. So was one eyebrow as well as his cheek. But none of it mattered because Danny was crying. Big Danny was curled on the path, clutching his chest, whimpering like a puppy.

The gang stood back amazed.

Danny rolled over and made as if to throw up on the tarmac but nothing came. The gang shuffled with embarrassment. Only when Danny propped himself on one knee and gasped "Help me up, you snotrags," did they crowd round him and lift him up. Tim heard one of them mutter "solar plexus" as they hobbled away.

Tim ran to save his skate tool from the road and slipped it comfortably back where it belonged, in his pocket. Years later he would sit on his own grandson's bed and tell him how Danny still shouted rude things at Tim from time to time because it would have been too much to expect that he'd do nothing. But Danny and the gang never dared hurt him, ever again.

"Thanks, Grandpa," he whispered, and did not stop running until he reached the pitch.

*   *   *

Tim walked into the kitchen and poured himself a huge glass of lemonade. It was due reward for a fantastic day. Not only had he defeated Danny once and for all, he had played the most dazzling football match of his life. They had won one-nil. Nothing over-marvellous about that, except that he, Tim, a new defender, had set up the goal with a kick more than half the length of the pitch. Not that it was worth telling Rox, who was busy doing nothing.

Since Monday when Jack had found the mice (all four dozen of them, now happily transported back to Mrs Baldock's) Rox had been preoccupied. It was so restful Tim hadn't bothered to ask why. So he was taken aback when she spoke first.

"Mum's got a job," she said. "On the phone. She's going to be Tiny Tim's mother in *A Christmas Carol*. We'll get loads of free tickets."

"Tim's mother?" Tim repeated. "Tiny *Tim's* mother? That's a . . ."

" . . . totally meaningless coincidence," Rox finished for him. "Listen, I've been thinking."

Tim gave her his shock-of-the-day face. "And what great thoughts have you been thinking?" he asked.

She took a red candle from the drawer.

"I . . . Well . . . I . . ." she said, and stopped.

Tim cleared his throat. He wanted to pin something down too but the words were hard to find. Rox put the candle in the middle of the table and struck a match. The scrape sounded unusually loud in the silence.

"Rox," he said, "I'm not really sure now if I saw a ghost for real or not. The more I think about it, the more I think I must have been asleep."

190

"Yeah," she said. "That's exactly what I think. Nightmares are nightmares. Coincidences happen. Simple as that, yeah?"

"Except . . ."

Tim's voice trailed away. He watched the match flame catch the pinkish wick. He longed to tell Rox how much he wanted his experience to have been a dream. But something very weird had happened. Something that could only be paranormal. It could not be explained any other way.

"I've still got bruises on my neck," he said softly.

"You did it to yourself in the dream," Rox said.

"Everybody smelt the fire."

"It was night time. We all dreamt the same."

"So how did I get into the secret room?"

"What?"

"I was in the secret room – through a wall. How did that happen?"

"Well, you must have been outside really and then when Dad broke in you ran past him. Simple."

"No," Tim said calmly. "It wasn't like that."

"Well, I don't care," Rox said, as Tim walked out. She gazed at the single flame until her eyes relaxed and it became two blurred ones, side by side. She had come to a decision.

She had had enough of magic and everything supernatural. It was all nonsense and love spells were the greatest nonsense of all. She wished with all her heart that they worked but ever since HE had found those mice – she refused even to think his name – he had not spoken a single word to her. Not one. Some

191

day she might fall in love with a person, and that person might fall in love with her, but it would have nothing to do with fox bones and Venus and the first Tuesday of the month. She took a deep breath and blew. The wick's glow faded from red-hot to black.

The doorbell buzzed. A whisper burst from her before she could suppress it, "Jack? Jack?"

She ran to the door.

Chapter Twenty-Nine

Rox stood for a second at the front door and imagined Jack — tall, tattooed and handsome — waiting on the other side. It had to be him. She pulled it wide open.

Mr MacFadyen bobbed on the doorstep, his arms full of red roses.

"Ah, I know I'm a little bit early but . . . "

Rox's eyes filled with tears, as she turned on her heels and trudged upstairs to throw herself on her bed. She had been right about the spells after all, and hated it.

Mr MacFadyen's lips puckered as if he'd been force-fed a lemon.

"Well really!" he muttered to Dad who'd come out to answer the door.

"You're looking smart, MacFadyen. She's upstairs, I think. Come in."

"I was hoping for a quick word with you as well," Mr MacFadyen said.

"You want to ask me for my mother-in-law's hand in marriage or something?" Dad smiled.

Mr MacFadyen blushed from his chin to the top of his head, "Eh . . . no."

Dad laughed. "How about a beer while we're waiting?" he said and led him into the sitting room. Both men sat by the fire. Mr MacFadyen's arm was lying firmly on his recovered clipboard.

"I'm so pleased to see this," he said. "I'm hopeless without it, you know."

Tim had suspected something big was afoot so he'd taken up his usual position behind the sofa.

"I'm pleased too," Dad said. "I thought that little loophole might work for you, so I e-mailed you as soon as it occurred to me."

"And it's all perfectly above board."

"Exactly."

What loophole? Tim thought. Must be the one they named after Dad.

"I'd been meaning to offer you the job for a while," Mr MacFadyen said. "It makes sense, doesn't it?"

"It will give me great pleasure," Dad smiled, "to be Aardvark Megabuild's accountant. I've had enough of my piggy little office in the City. It's just as well really with the vellum sheets being worthless."

"Not quite worthless," Mr MacFadyen said, "but twentieth-century definitely. Sorry you got your hopes up but I did have another look at my colleague's records. We didn't bother much before, as they were too recent. Most of the abbey isn't that old, you know. Parts of it are, but the chapel and Tim's room, are Edwardian."

"Which Edward?" Dad asked.

"Edward the Seventh, I'm afraid. The one who came after Queen Victoria in 1901. After Henry VIII did his stuff destroying all the abbeys around Britain, Greenwich Abbey lay in ruins until 1912. Twelve monks got together at that point to rebuild it. They were keen on living the real Medieval life. Stone beds and so on. Proper bread. They didn't get far."

Something tingled up Tim's spine. He crawled into the hall and called Rox. Swathed in black, she glided from her room onto the landing.

"What?" she spat.

"Come here, you have to hear this. It's about when the abbey was built."

They listened together from behind the door.

"The records are sketchy," Mr MacFadyen was saying. "The local newspapers are the best we've got, and it looks as if the monks were all watching an eclipse one night when the abbey burned down. Most of it anyway. Candle fire probably. It happened a lot in those days and the survivors hadn't the money or the strength to rebuild. Nobody would have anything to do with the place after that. People said it was cursed. The estate agents didn't mention it to you, I dare say."

"They did not," Dad frowned. "What kind of curse?"

Mr MacFadyen smoothed his blue silk tie.

"To do with the corpses, I expect," he replied.

In two strides Rox was standing in the room like a furious crow.

"What corpses?" she demanded.

"Yeah," Tim said, following her into the room.

"Two bodies," Mr MacFadyen said, "were found in your secret room. Which wasn't a secret room then, it was a side-room to the chapel. They were taken away for burial and the builders sealed it off."

"Two bodies? Rox repeated, "two monks? Two monks!"

"Who were they?" Tim dared to ask. His heart was in overdrive.

"Yeah," Rox said, "Was one a baker and one a scribe? Were they fighting?"

"I'm sorry," Mr MacFadyen was looking lost in this avalanche of questions, "I have no idea!"

Dad came to his rescue, "Steady on, kids, how would Mr MacFadyen know?" But even he couldn't resist it.

"Just the two bodies?" he asked, as if it was a perfectly normal question, like just two sugars in your tea?

"Well, yes," Mr MacFadyen replied, "The rest were outside watching the eclipse, weren't they? That's all I can tell you." He sipped his beer nervously.

Rox swept over to Dad and took a bow.

"Now will you believe me?" She said, glaring at Dad.

Dad sat up straight as if he'd just understood the theory of relativity, or in this case understood his own son and daughter.

"Your dreams, Rox — about the artist and the inks and loaves," he stuttered, "and Tim — your ghost, the baker!" He slapped his own forehead. "That's what the fire chief meant. And Mrs Baldock! She knew too! You did activate a ghost"

"*Two* ghosts," Tim cut in quietly.

"But you never meant to!" Dad went on. "You poor loves, is it possible? Hang on, tell me it all again, slowly. No," he sighed, "come here first. Both of you."

He stood up and pulled Rox and Tim close to him. Soon they were having the biggest three-way hug in the world.

When the front door slammed, they all jumped apart as if they'd been electrocuted. But it was only Mum and Georgie back from the supermarket.

"Look what I found!" Mum called from the hall.

"No more surprises please!" Rox groaned and flopped in a chair. Dad drained his drink just in time as Georgie barged in and plonked himself on his knee.

Mum came in, said hello to Mr MacFayden and put a glasses case in Tim's hand. A familiar glasses case.

"Your spares," she said, "they were in the car all the time. Hiding under the seat. No wonder I couldn't find them."

"You were looking?" Tim asked.

"Of course! I do try, you know." Then Mum hugged him too. "Why didn't you tell me they were missing?" she asked.

Tim didn't bother to say that he had. Mum looked round at all the stunned faces. "What?" she asked.

Dad sat her down and said, "We-e-ell . . ."

Tim and Rox both wanted to tell her at once. There was a jumble of both of them shouting and laughing and trying to get a word in as they each told their side of the story. Gradually, like the moment when the moon completely covers the sun in an eclipse, there was a sense of everything fitting perfectly and they both went, "Yes!"

The door opened again.

"Ah! Here she is at last," said Mr MacFadyen.

Gran walked in wearing a pink and green dress and sparkly jewellery.

"You look marvellous, old thing," Dad said, kissing her cheek.

"Less of the old, thank you, Tony. What's all the noise about?"

"I'll tell you in the car, my dear." Mr MacFadyen had shot to his feet. "And I'm not sure you're going to believe it."

Rox moved behind her and whispered, "Isn't he a bit young for you, Gran?"

"Rubbish!" Gran replied loudly. "Brian appreciates *anno domini*. That's Latin for what the years can bring. Right, Brian?"

Mr MacFadyen thrust the roses at her. Gran glanced anxiously at Mum.

Mum pursed her lips, then kissed Gran's cheek and wished her a lovely time.

But Gran's not that keen on ballet, Tim thought. *She's going to hate every minute.*

Chapter Thirty

Tim was gliding on his skateboard through the park thinking that Sundays were even better than Saturdays. Once your homework was out of the way, you could skateboard all day. He stopped to let Georgie and Gran catch up. They'd been to the shops to buy Gran a new shirt.

"How was the ballet?" Tim asked her. He was hoping to find a moment when he could break it to her sensitively that Grandpa's skate tool had got badly squashed by the enemy and would never be the same again. Gran gazed across the river at Canary Wharf Tower glowing bronze in the evening light.

"It was okay," she smiled, "except for all the galumph-ing about. Honestly! Why do they have to do it all on tiptoes? Couldn't they just get taller people? I would never have dared say so to your Grandpa," she laughed.

Tim grinned as Gran went on.

"But the fact is I can't stand ballet. I only ever went to please Desmond and last night I went to please Brian, Mr MacFadyen, who is otherwise a reasonably sensible person," she said.

Gran opened her shopping bag and pulled out her new shirt. She held its red checks against her chest.

"From now on," she said, "I'm going to please myself and go line-dancing."

"What?" Tim and Georgie shouted together.

Tim was shocked. "Grandpa will be turning in his urn!" he said.

"Maybe," Gran grinned. "You still got that poetry book of his?"

Tim pulled it out of his back pocket. It was a useful place to keep it in case he had to sit down suddenly while skateboarding.

Gran opened it tenderly.

"He loved this bit, listen," she said, *"Faeries . . ."*

Tim and Georgie snorted.

"Stop it now," she said, crossly. "It's your Grandpa's favourite." They calmed down to broad grins as Gran read,

" *. . . come take me out of this dull world.*
For I would ride with you upon the wind,
Run on the top of this dishevelled tide
And dance upon the mountains like a flame."

She sniffed and buried her head in the new shirt.

Georgie started to snigger, until Tim shoved him and he stopped.

"So," she said, looking up, "Brian and I are going line-dancing next week. You do it yourself. Much more fun. I might not look like it but inside I'll be dancing like a flame."

She tripped a few sideways steps. "And I'll be thinking about your Grandpa. I still adore him, you know. And he's still with me."

"He's dead, Gran," Georgie said.

"I know he is, darling," Gran smiled, "but he's not gone, is he? He's here," she put one hand on her heart and the other on Georgie's, "and here. All the time."

Tim loved to talk about Grandpa like this. After Grandpa died, people were afraid to talk about him. It was as if he'd turned frightening, like some sort of ghost or something. But he wasn't. Tim still wasn't really sure if there were ghosts or not, but one thing he did know was that Grandpa was with him, dead but not gone. He was with all of them, Mum too. As soon as they got back Tim was going to give Mum a hug and tell her so. They couldn't touch Grandpa's love or prod it or hug it but it was solid all the same.

"He's with me too, Gran," Tim said as he bent forward a little, the way Grandpa used to on his skates. He straightened up. Now was the moment.

"Gran," Tim said, pulling Grandpa's spanner from his pocket, "Big Danny's lot were using it for steam-roller practice."

"Never mind," Gran smiled, hugging him. She lightly kissed the spanner.

"Give it here," she said, "that skateboard of yours."

Gran upended Tim's skateboard and slid the spanner over the kingpin nut at a slight angle, as if she'd been doing it all her life. A couple of yanks and the trucks tightened. Tim's speed wobble problems were over.

"Perfect," Tim smiled, and they all headed for home.